THE BLACKSTONE CHRONICLES

PART 6
ASYLUM

John Saul

FAWCETT CREST • NEW YORK

A Fawcett Crest Book
Published by Ballantine Books
Copyright © 1997 by John Saul
Excerpt from *The Presence* copyright © 1997 by John Saul

http://www.randomhouse.com

Library of Congress Catalog Card Number: 97-90040

ISBN 0-449-22794-4

Manufactured in the United States of America

First Edition: July 1997

10 9 8 7 6 5 4 3 2 1

For six chilling months you have lived in the New England town of Blackstone, witnessing the dark wrath of an unspeakable evil, a menacing force unleashed from deep within the old Asylum. Mysterious gifts seemed to appear out of the shadows for unsuspecting recipients. Each told a horrifying story . . .

In Part 1, an "innocent" antique doll tore apart the young family of the local contractor, Bill McGuire.

In Part 2, Jules Hartwick, the town's bank president, saw a silver locket spur a murderous, maniacal rage.

In Part 3, Rebecca Morrison watched in horror as a dragon-shaped cigarette lighter ignited a fiery and very deadly reunion.

In Part 4, the librarian, Germaine Wagner, clutched a linen handkerchief and was soon enmeshed in a terrifying nightmare.

In Part 5, an antique stereoscope conjured attorney Ed Becker's horrific memories to three-dimensional life . . . and brought grisly death.

Now enter the very heart of terror, and experience the explosive conclusion . . .

THE BLACKSTONE CHRONICLES
ASYLUM

By John Saul:

SUFFER THE CHILDREN
PUNISH THE SINNERS
CRY FOR THE STRANGERS
COMES THE BLIND FURY
WHEN THE WIND BLOWS
THE GOD PROJECT
NATHANIEL
BRAINCHILD
HELLFIRE
THE UNWANTED
THE UNLOVED
CREATURE
SECOND CHILD
SLEEPWALK
DARKNESS
SHADOWS
GUARDIAN*
THE HOMING*
BLACK LIGHTNING*
THE BLACKSTONE CHRONICLES:
    Part 1—AN EYE FOR AN EYE: THE DOLL*
    Part 2—TWIST OF FATE: THE LOCKET*
    Part 3—ASHES TO ASHES:
       THE DRAGON'S FLAME*
    Part 4—IN THE SHADOW OF EVIL:
       THE HANDKERCHIEF*
    Part 5—DAY OF RECKONING:
       THE STEREOSCOPE*
    Part 6—ASYLUM*

Published by Fawcett Books

*For Linda, now
and in the future*

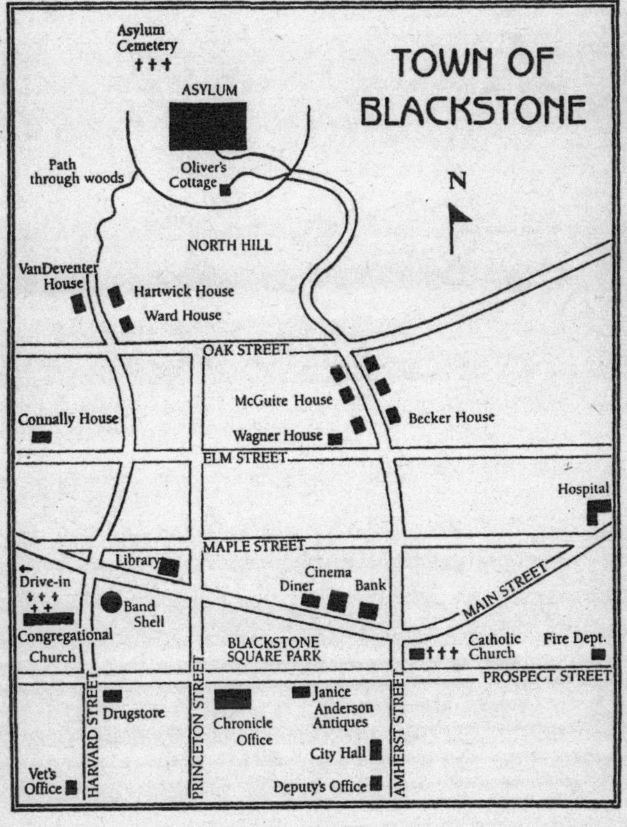

TOWN OF BLACKSTONE
N
Asylum Cemetery
ASYLUM
Oliver's Cottage
Path through woods
NORTH HILL
VanDeventer House
Hartwick House
Ward House
Connally House
OAK STREET
McGuire House
Becker House
Wagner House
ELM STREET
Hospital
MAPLE STREET
Library
Cinema
Drive-in
Diner
Bank
MAIN STREET
Band Shell
Congregational Church
BLACKSTONE SQUARE PARK
Catholic Church
Fire Dept.
PROSPECT STREET
HARVARD STREET
Drugstore
PRINCETON STREET
Chronicle Office
Janice Anderson Antiques
City Hall
AMHERST STREET
Vet's Office
Deputy's Office

The Connally Family

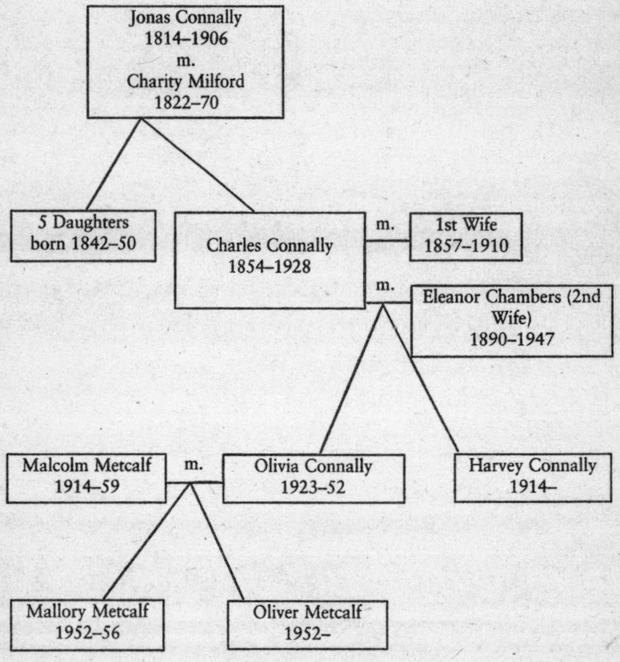

ASYLUM

Prelude

Night lay over Blackstone like a heavy, suffocating shroud, but it was not merely the darkness that had driven the town's citizens from Main and Elm streets, from the locked and shuttered library and the cozy camaraderie of the Red Hen.

Fear, as well as night, now held the people of Blackstone in its clutches. Terror had spread through the village like a virus, infecting first one person, and then another, until at last no one had escaped its icy touch.

Every night when they locked their doors, the people of Blackstone prayed that this would not be the night when evil came to prey on them. If it had to feed, let it find succor within someone else's walls, destroy the lives of someone else's family.

The fever of fear was no longer limited to the hours of darkness, for even in the bright sunshine of a springtime afternoon, there wasn't a soul in Blackstone who couldn't feel his neighbors' eyes watching. Watching, and wondering.

Who would be next?

And how would it come?

The universal custom of honoring birthdays and anniversaries with gifts had abruptly stopped in Blackstone, for everyone in town had heard that any object, even the most innocent-seeming gift, could carry the curse—a doll, a handkerchief, a silver locket—*anything* could bring home the reign of terror.

The flea market had been abandoned, for everyone had heard about the dragon-shaped lighter that Rebecca Morrison had given to her cousin. Janice Anderson hadn't seen a customer in a week. The post office had begun returning packages of every description to their senders, all of them marked with the same message: DELIVERY REFUSED.

Every day the tension grew, and soon families who had been neighbors and friends for more generations than they could remember were looking at one another with undisguised suspicion. But it was at night that nerves jumped and heartbeats hammered, at night when everyone retreated to their homes and tried to bar their doors against fear. Behind their locks and barricades they knew precautions were useless, of course, for deep in their souls, each of them understood that if the madness came to invade his home, no locks would keep it out, no shutters hold it at bay.

It would slither in through the crevices and cracks, and by morning—

But none of them wanted to think about morning.

Just to get through the night was enough.

And this night—a night filled with moonless blackness made palpable by heavy fog—was the worst of all. On most other nights the people of Blackstone had been able to peek from their windows, searching the pools of light around the street lamps for signs of danger.

Tonight there was only darkness, and the viscous mist that turned keen eyes blind.

Through the fog and darkness a single figure moved, slipping unseen from the door of the Asylum, its cloak thrown loose around its shoulders. It drifted through the ebony night with wraithlike grace, a presence that crept from house to house.

In every house, the figure caught a glimpse of terror as it peered unseen through a forgotten shade or slightly parted curtain with a perfect, sinuous stealth that never betrayed its presence for an instant. The watcher could almost smell the fear, and shivers of excitement ran over its skin like a lover's fingers. Moving, silently stalking. A shadow that briefly crossed from one window to the next. Savoring the suffering. Delighting in the disease it had unleashed upon the town.

It was close to dawn when finally the triumphal tour was near an end, and the figure came to the house upon whose step it would leave its most important gift.

At this house, the figure lingered long, gazing up at the darkened windows from which no light spilled. There was no movement within, nor was there the scent of fear that issued from every other house it had visited. As the cloaked intruder circled this house, rage began to build inside it, until, reflecting upon the vengeance this gift would wreak upon this house's only occupant, the fury slowly ebbed away, leaving in its place a shiver of strangely erotic excitement.

Soon, soon, the wrath would descend upon this place too.

Caressing the gift one last time, the dark figure laid it lovingly at the front door, then faded into the blackness as silently as it had come.

Chapter 1

Numb.

Every part of Rebecca Morrison seemed to have gone numb.

A chill had crept over her that she'd never experienced before. She had always known what it felt like to be cold, of course, for growing up in New Hampshire meant winters wading through snowbanks and temperatures that sank far below zero. When she was a little girl, she loved those days. Her mother would bundle her up in a thick woolen snowsuit, and put mittens on her hands and a stocking cap on her head, and Rebecca would hurl herself into the snowy paradise outside with an excitement that sometimes made her feel like she would simply burst with joy. She would flop down into the snow, wave her arms and spread her legs, then jump up to admire the angel she had made. Sometimes she'd even leap right into a big drift and bury her face in the cold white cottony fluff because the frozen, wet purity was so refreshing, its aftertingle so deliciously shivery. Best of all were "snow days," when school was closed, grown-ups stayed inside their warm kitchens, and she would go off in search of other kids to play with. Inevitably, she'd wind up in a snowball fight that—equally—required her to shed her mittens since everyone knew you couldn't make a proper snowball with mittens on. By the time the grown-ups came to chase everyone inside, Rebecca's fingers would be freezing, and snow would have worked its way inside her sleeves as well. The cold she'd felt then had been an exciting cold, a happy, carefree cold that always vanished deliciously with a cup of hot cocoa covered with marshmallows, sipped in front of the fire blazing in the living room hearth of her parents' house on Maple Street.

There had been other kinds of cold, though, that hadn't been nearly as much fun.

The cold she'd felt when there weren't enough blankets on the bed and Aunt Martha turned the thermostat low, to save money and save Rebecca's "spendthrift soul."

The icy cold of the first dip into the quarry in spring, when the water was barely above freezing.

The clammy chill when she'd gotten caught in a rainstorm with neither raincoat nor umbrella to protect her from getting soaked through to the skin.

That kind of cold, though, could be banished with an extra comforter, or a thick terry-cloth towel, or a change into dry clothes.

Even the chill of a fever that could rattle her teeth and turn her skin clammy was nothing like what she was feeling now, for even when she'd been in a fever's grip, she always knew it was only a temporary thing, that in a few hours, perhaps even a day, it would pass and she would feel warm again.

The cold she felt now had crept up on her so slowly that she couldn't really remember when it began; indeed, it was as if it had always been there. Every part of her body either had gone so numb that she had no feeling at all or ached with a dull pain, an ache that had burrowed into every muscle, spread through every bone. She wasn't frozen; she knew that. She could still move her arms and legs, still twist her neck and flex her back. But every movement was agonizing, every twitch of every muscle over which she had managed to retain control brought her a new sensation of pain.

The cold had even seeped into her mind, slowing her wits and confusing her so badly that she was no longer sure when she was awake and when she was sleeping; could not determine which of the sensations she felt were real, and which were the products of the dark nightmares that seized her whenever she slept.

It was the cold of death.

Rebecca knew that, knew it with a strange certainty that had grown in her mind until she'd all but given up any hope of surviving the ordeal that began when she'd fled from Germaine Wagner's house.

How long had it been?

She had no idea, for time itself no longer meant anything to her.

Not only was there no longer any distinction between night and day, but the difference between a minute and an hour, a day and a week, a month and a year, had disappeared. An hour might be a lifetime, and a month no more than a minute.

It didn't matter, for in the world into which Rebecca had plummeted—if it was this world at all—there was no longer any time.

Only cold.

The cold of the grave.

There were times when she thought she must have

died, when the darkness around her was so deep that she knew she must be buried in the earth. But then some brief sensation would penetrate the numbing cold; a sound perhaps, or a sharp twinge of pain that would rouse her, however briefly, from the strange not-quite-sleep into which she'd sunk.

For a while she tried to keep track of the passing time, tried to count the seconds that had turned into small eternities, but even that had become impossible, for there was no way to remember how many seconds she'd counted, no way to mark the passing minutes and hours.

The Tormentor—that was how she thought of her captor now, as almost an abstraction of a being, rather than a man with a face hidden by darkness and a personality concealed by silence. The Tormentor came and went, and Rebecca had long since ceased to feel any reaction to him.

Not surprise.

Not terror.

Not even apprehension anymore.

At first, in a time grown dim and distant in her memory, she had feared his coming, her heart pounding when she heard his scraping step or even sensed his presence when no sound betrayed that he was there.

He brought her food and water, though, for which she was grateful, though his whispered words made her flesh crawl no less than did his touch. But as the cold had tunneled deeper within her mind and her body and her spirit, Rebecca even stopped thinking about what it might be that he wanted from her, what reason he might have had for bringing her here.

Now, as her mind rose slowly out of the black pit of sleep, and the cold-induced nightmares loosened their grip, she sensed that he was there once more. It was nothing in the darkness that betrayed his presence; no sound of footsteps or rasping breath, no whispered words murmured in her ear, no touch of gloved fingers on her flesh.

Only a sense that she was not alone.

Then there was a minute lessening of the darkness, and like a flower turning toward the sun, she found herself turning her head, an involuntary groping for the source of the faint brightening that slightly grayed her world of darkness.

Then there was a new sensation.

Arms were picking her up. As she was lifted off the floor on which she lay, every nerve and muscle in her body screamed in protest, and a cry of anguished agony rose in her throat.

For an instant she tried to open her mouth to give vent to the erupting scream, but a tearing pain in her lips reminded her of the tape that covered her mouth. With a surge of sudden determination she managed to control her scream before it could back up in her throat, choke and strangle her and make her retch, and fill her mouth and nose with burning bile. As the wave of pain crashed over her and finally began to ebb, her cry of agonized protest emerged as nothing more than a stifled and sighing moan.

Held tightly in the Tormentor's grasp, she felt herself being carried out of the room that had been her prison, and though she could see nothing through the tape blindfold, she had a sense of walls that were close at hand on either side, and knew with an instinctive certainty that she was being borne down a long corridor. The Tormentor's pace changed, and Rebecca had a vague sensation of rising.

Stairs! She was being carried up a flight of stairs.

Another corridor, but, oddly, she sensed that this one was wider than the other, that the spaces here were larger. But how could she know? The darkness around her was only a nearly imperceptible shade lighter than the blackness into which she'd been sunk for so long.

And yet something was different.

Something had changed.

Something was about to happen.

Something terrible.

Chapter 2

*I*t was a glorious spring morning. Under normal circumstances, Oliver Metcalf would have been humming to himself as he fixed his first cup of coffee, glanced through the *Manchester Guardian*, then set off for the office, savoring every breath of the sweet air. A day when he might have paused to watch the baby robins tumbling across the lawn in front of Bill McGuire's house as their parents hopped anxiously around, cheeping their encouragement while the chicks struggled through their first clumsy flight lessons. A day when he would have dawdled at the Red Hen over an extra cup of coffee before heading to the *Chronicle* office; a sunshiny, optimistic morning that might induce him to wonder if this would be the day that Rebecca Morrison agreed to let him take her out to dinner.

On a day like today he might even have planned a run down to Boston. But this morning, as on every morning since Rebecca disappeared, Oliver was barely aware of the fresh April breeze or the new buds on the venerable elms outside his kitchen window. From the moment he'd awakened from a restless sleep that had been disturbed by nightmares he couldn't quite remember— vaguely horrible dreams he wasn't sure he *wanted* to remember—dire thoughts of what might have happened to Rebecca were already churning through his mind. He was still trying to hold to the hope that Germaine Wagner's terrible accident had upset Rebecca so much that she'd simply fled from it. But as the days dragged by, and his heart had filled with expectation every time the phone rang, only to deflate with disappointment when it was not Rebecca's voice each time he picked it up, it was becoming harder and harder to cling to the faith that Rebecca would return to Blackstone—and to him— unharmed.

Surely, if she was all right, she would have called him. Unless what she'd witnessed in the Wagners' house had been so horrifying that she simply blocked it, and every-thing else, out of her memory. Except that Oliver knew just how rare amnesia really was—far more common, in fact, in romance novels and cheap thrillers than it was in real life. Unable to fly directly in the face of logic, he had finally admitted to himself that she must be in danger, perhaps deadly danger. That thought led directly to a depression into which he was sinking deeper every day. Although with every dawn that had broken since her dis-appearance, Oliver told himself that today he would at last hear from her, the self-assurances had long since begun to ring hollow.

Still, he was resolutely unwilling to grant any credi-bility to the people who thought Rebecca had finally turned on Germaine. Like everyone in town, Oliver was aware of how badly Germaine Wagner had treated Rebecca. But deep in his heart he was certain that Rebecca was incapable of violence. No, it would have been much more like Rebecca to pity Germaine for the woman's unhappiness than to turn on her for her meanness of spirit.

All that was left, then, was that something terrible had befallen Rebecca. That thought—and his inability to do anything to help her—now weighed so heavily on Oliver that he was finding it more and more difficult even to get out of bed in the morning. The combined effects of his sleepless tossing and turning, and the nightmares that plagued him when he did sleep, were taking their toll. This morning, he had almost decided to call Lois and tell her he wouldn't be in. Yet the prospect of staying alone in his house all day was even less appealing, so finally, shoulders stooped with the weight of his worry, he set out down Amherst Street toward the village.

The walk did little to pick up his spirits. Crossing Oak, he came to the part of Amherst Street where both the McGuires and the Beckers lived, and saw Megan McGuire sitting on the swing that hung from the lowest branch of an enormous oak tree in her front yard. He stopped for a moment intending to talk to her, and called out, "Good morning." At first she didn't seem to hear him. When he called her name, she looked sharply up at him, then got off the swing and started toward him, cradling a doll in her arms.

The doll that had been an anonymous gift, either for her or for the baby her mother had been about to deliver when Elizabeth McGuire had miscarried.

"It hurts every time I look at it," Bill McGuire had told Oliver a few weeks before. "But I can't bring myself to take the damn thing away from her. Since Elizabeth died, she keeps it with her all the time. Even takes it to school with her. I talked to Phil Margolis about it, but he says I should just let her be, at least for a while." The pain had misted Bill's eyes, and his voice had cracked. "Of course, that's what he said about Elizabeth too," he went on. "But I shouldn't have let her be. I should have stayed with her, every minute."

Oliver had tried to reassure him. "You can't blame yourself, Bill. All of us are responsible for our own lives, but not for other people's. And Elizabeth was . . ." He hadn't finished his sentence, but he hadn't needed to.

"Delicate?" Bill had asked, his tone tinged with bitterness. "Isn't that what Edna Burnham always says? That Elizabeth was 'delicate'?" He'd shaken his head. "She got through her sister's breakdown when she was a child, and she got through the loss of her parents a few years later. If you're 'delicate,' you don't survive tragedies like that. But losing the baby was just too much for her, and I should have known that. I should have known not to leave her alone that morning."

Unlike her father, whose grief had not abated, Megan seemed to Oliver to have sublimated her sorrow by focusing entirely on the doll, which she was clutching protectively even now, as she crossed the lawn toward him. He supposed Phil Margolis was right, and that given enough time, Megan would emerge from the shell she seemed to have formed around herself and the doll. As Megan walked slowly toward the sidewalk where he stood, Oliver could see her lips moving as she whispered to the doll.

"How are you today, Megan?" Oliver asked as the little girl stopped a few feet away from him.

"I'm all right," Megan replied. "Sam and I were playing on the swing."

" 'Sam,' " Oliver repeated. "Why did you name him Sam?"

Megan's eyes instantly darkened. "Sam's a girl," she said. "We don't like boys."

"I see," Oliver said gravely. "May I hold Sam?"

Megan shook her head. "Nobody can hold Sam but me," she said. "She's my friend, and I'm her friend, and she hates everyone else." She looked lovingly down into the doll's face. "Isn't that right, Sam?" A moment later, as if the doll had spoken to her, Megan looked up at Oliver again. "Sam wants you to go away now," she announced. "She wants you to leave us alone."

Oliver hesitated, but suddenly there was a look in Megan's eyes such as he'd never seen in a child before.

Evil.

The word rose up in his mind and took Oliver by surprise, like a right hook to the jaw. Astonished, he recovered himself to see that the demon-flash was gone. But Megan stared steadily at him, and under the child's relentless gaze it was finally he who shifted his eyes from hers.

"I'm sorry," he heard himself say, almost as if the words were coming from someone else. "I didn't mean to—" He stopped, aware that he'd been about to apologize for having *bothered* Megan. How ridiculous that he, an adult, should feel the need to apologize to this little girl merely for having spoken a few friendly words!

Worse, why did the way she was staring at him upset him so?

Saying nothing more to her, Oliver turned and continued down Amherst Street.

A moment later he was across from the Becker house. It was empty now. Bonnie and Amy had moved down to Boston, where Ed was still in intensive care. Three vertebrae in his neck had been shattered in his fall the night of the explosion in the basement, and though Ed was still alive, he was dependent on a respirator to breathe for him, and had yet to speak a word since the accident. The doctors assured Bonnie that in time he would be able to talk again, but when Oliver had gone down to Boston the day before yesterday to see Ed, he'd wondered if the doctors had told Bonnie the truth. Though Ed had been awake—Oliver had seen his eyes blink several times during the half hour he sat with Ed—he hadn't been certain whether Ed even knew he was there, much less recognized him. There was a look in the attorney's eyes—a gaze that, though not vacant, had not been focused on him either. Ed Becker appeared to have wandered into some other world, a universe buried so deep within his own mind that he was unable to find his way back to the plane of ordinary life in which he had existed before his accident.

When Oliver left the ICU, Bonnie told him about the dreams Ed had been having—dreams Ed had claimed were coming true—and about the stereoscope they'd found in the chest of drawers that Ed brought down from the Asylum.

"I keep thinking about those gifts everyone's been talking about," Bonnie said, her eyes looking almost as haunted as her husband's. "Except the stereoscope wasn't a gift at all—it just happened to be in one of the drawers in that old dresser."

Bonnie had told him about the pictures too, and when he returned to Blackstone, Oliver, curious, had gone to their house, entering with the keys she'd provided, to look for the stereoscope and view the pictures.

He'd found no trace either of the stereoscope or of the photographs Bonnie—and Amy too—had described to him. They had vanished as thoroughly as if they'd never existed, though Bonnie had directed him to the coffee table in the living room, where, she said, they'd been on the night that Ed had fallen. Oliver had searched everywhere, but they were nowhere to be found. The house itself had taken on an odd feeling of abandonment, as if it knew that Bonnie had decided she would never set foot in it again. "It isn't just what happened to Ed," she'd insisted. "I just don't think I'd ever feel safe there again. Not after the explosion. I'd never get a wink of sleep in that house. And I could never let Amy sleep there again."

But it was more than that, Oliver suspected. Bonnie, like so many other people in town, had become convinced that somehow, in some way she didn't understand, an evil force had invaded Blackstone.

There was that word again. *Evil.* The same word that had popped into his mind when he'd encountered Megan McGuire a few moments ago. But the word hadn't simply come into Oliver's mind this time. It was the word that Bonnie Becker herself had used to describe the events that had resulted in her husband's paralysis, and almost killed her and her daughter as well.

It wasn't just the house Bonnie Becker wasn't coming back to.

It was the town too.

"My family is in Boston and all my friends are here," she'd said. "I don't have any reason to go back to Blackstone." She'd hesitated, but then finished the thought. "And frankly, I don't understand why anyone would stay there, after everything that's happened." Then she had whispered the word once more. "Evil. Something evil is going on there."

Now, in the warmth of the April morning, Oliver Metcalf shivered slightly, as if a chilly presence had touched him. Of course, it couldn't possibly be true, but on the other hand . . .

He found himself counting the tragedies that had befallen his friends:

The suicide of Jules Hartwick, which he'd witnessed himself.

The burning of Martha Ward's house, in which Martha had perished and Rebecca had nearly been killed.

And the horror perpetrated in Germaine Wagner's house—Germaine's body crushed beneath the elevator, her elderly wheelchair-bound mother trapped inside the cage and felled by a massive stroke—the night Rebecca had vanished.

Oliver knew that it wasn't just Bonnie Becker who was whispering about a curse that had befallen Blackstone. The rumors were rampaging through the town like a disease, and everywhere he went, he could feel everyone watching everyone else, as if searching for some sign—some mark—that would tell them who might be next.

There were explanations—reasonable explanations—for everything that had happened in Blackstone. There had to be. And he would find them.

But of one thing he was certain.

There was no evil, no curse. Things like that simply didn't exist.

And yet, as he continued down the hill into the village and started across the square toward the *Chronicle* office, he found himself turning to gaze back at the Asylum, looming above the town as it had for nearly a century. And he found himself thinking once more about the outrages that he now knew had been practiced within its walls. *That* was evil—evil that cloaked itself in the guise of medical science.

If such an evil could prevail, an evil that could turn the Hippocratic oath to acts of unspeakable horror, then perhaps evil *did* exist and could inhabit other forms, take on other unknowable black shapes.

Turning away from the Asylum's brooding stare just as he'd turned away from Megan McGuire's gaze a few minutes ago, Oliver tried to put the unsettling idea out of his mind.

He couldn't.

The seed was planted. Already, it was starting to grow.

Chapter 3

By the time Harvey Connally had entered his ninth decade, he'd discovered two truths: the first was that what most people thought of as the wisdom that comes with age was in reality little more than the realization that most things, if left to their own devices, will take care of themselves. That first truth had led directly to the second one: that very little ever needed to be done right away, and that it was therefore always best to think things over carefully before taking any action. Thus, when he found the package sitting on his front porch that morning, resting next to his copy of the *Manchester Guardian*—which, though in his opinion not nearly as good a paper as his nephew's *Blackstone Chronicle*, at least had the virtue of coming out on a daily basis—he chose to ignore the plainly wrapped box, at least for the moment. Retrieving the newspaper, he left the package on the porch while he went to the kitchen, fixed himself the first of the two cups of coffee he always drank in the morning—the stingy ration of caffeine that was all that Phil Margolis approved—and perused the *Guardian*. He avoided the editorial page since editorials had the habit of arousing enough outrage in him to bring on a stroke. With his second cup of coffee, though, he folded the paper and finally allowed his attention to turn to the package that still lay on his front porch. He'd noted that it bore no stamps, and no address, so he knew it must have been delivered sometime during the night.

Harvey Connally did not approve of people skulking about in the dark, leaving anonymous packages on other people's front porches. Yet the moment he'd seen the parcel, he'd immediately thought of Rebecca Morrison's claim that she'd seen someone in Jules Hartwick's driveway the night before he killed himself. He recalled the package that had been delivered to the McGuires' a few days before Elizabeth died. "Gifts" that Edna Burnham had declared to be the harbingers of evil.

Harvey Connally had no more patience with harbingers of evil than he had with skulkers in the night.

Whatever had happened to all those people, he was certain, had more to do with their own failings than with evil being visited upon them from some unknown source.

And yet . . .

And yet led Harvey Connally to an unaccustomed third cup of coffee. As he savored every forbidden sip of it, he found himself pondering the idea of Divine Retribution. It was a concept in which Harvey, at least until recently, had put no faith whatsoever. However, over the past few weeks, as he'd watched tragedy strike one after another of Blackstone's oldest families, he'd begun to wonder.

Every family to whom one of the mysterious "gifts" had been delivered had some connection to the Asylum, and each of the tragedies had contained elements that eerily paralleled events that had occurred in Blackstone's past. Harvey had first noted such an uncanny parallel when Jules Hartwick had disemboweled himself on the steps of the Asylum. Though everyone had agreed that it was the investigation of the bank by the Federal Reserve that triggered Jules's breakdown and suicide, Harvey had instead focused on the insane jealousy Jules had exhibited toward his wife that day.

The same raging jealousy, in fact, that Harvey remembered Jules's father exhibiting half a century ago when Hartwick had become convinced that his wife was having an affair with Malcolm Metcalf. But the elder Hartwick hadn't killed himself. Instead he had merely warned his wife that if the affair continued, he would divorce her, and make the reason for the divorce public. He had promptly banished the portrait of Louisa in her Gray Lady apron—which Harvey now suspected she intended as a gift to her lover—to the attic. And that had been that. Louisa had never again gone anywhere near the Asylum. When Malcolm Metcalf died, the Hartwicks had been conspicuous by their absence from his burial.

After making that connection, Harvey had begun to listen carefully to everything that had been said about the recent deaths in Blackstone. One by one, he began putting the pieces together. He remembered the child to whom Bill McGuire's great-aunt Laurette had given birth, a child who had disappeared into the Asylum one day, never to be seen again. It hadn't been long before Laurette, despondent at the loss of her child, had drowned while vacationing at Cape Cod. Her death had of course been attributed to an accident, but Harvey had long ago concluded that even if Laurette hadn't planned to die, neither had she done anything to save herself. Elizabeth McGuire's loss of her baby son and subsequent fatal fall seemed to Harvey a circumstance far too eerily similar to be merely coincidental.

As the months went by, each new tragedy stirred a

memory within Harvey Connally. At last, he'd become convinced that Blackstone's misfortunes were, indeed, connected to the Asylum. It was as if the sins of the fathers were being visited on the sons; as if the hand of God was finally reaching out to strike down the descendants of those whose transgressions had been hidden away within the Asylum's cold stone rooms.

Divine Retribution.

Except that Harvey Connally's mind, trained in the rigors of rationalist thought, wouldn't accept the idea of Divine Retribution. While the rest of Blackstone buzzed with speculation and gossip, Harvey Connally kept his own counsel, listening, always listening, but contributing nothing to the gushing torrent of rumor that flooded the town. Instead he quietly processed each item of news or speculation through his own mind, analyzing every theory he heard, discarding the most outlandish ideas, and filing away the bits and pieces that he couldn't dismiss, as if they were the jagged parts of a complicated jigsaw puzzle and the picture would come clear once he had all the pieces gathered and sorted.

But it had not come clear. For no matter how he tried to fit the pieces together, the only shape that ever emerged, superimposed upon Harvey's mental image of Blackstone's historical landscape, was a fuzzy vision of Malcolm Metcalf, a man who had been dead for nearly half of Harvey Connally's life.

But Harvey did not believe in ghosts any more than he believed in Divine Retribution.

When he finished the third cup of coffee, he slowly returned to the front porch, stooped stiffly down, and picked up the package. Holding the parcel carefully, he took it to his study, set it on his desk, and examined it from every angle. Finding no clue as to its origin, nor anything that he would consider a distinguishing mark, he momentarily entertained the idea of calling young Steven Driver, but dismissed the thought almost immediately: there was far too great a possibility that the sheriff's deputy would, on the pretext of protecting him, confiscate the contents. That issue decided, Harvey Connally carefully opened the package, doing as little damage to the paper in which it was wrapped as he could. As the wrapping fell away, the old man found himself gazing at an object of a kind he hadn't seen in years.

He recognized it instantly. It was an old-fashioned razor case, very much like the one his father had owned when Harvey was a boy. Instinctively, he reached out to caress the box, just as he had when he was a small boy and his father had told him he could touch the case, but never open it. Now, as the old man's fingers traced the pattern of ivory and ebony that had been inlaid into the box's mahogany lid, a profusion of memories was unleashed in his mind. He saw himself back in the bathroom of the house on Amherst Street where he'd grown up, his mother having refused to live in the enormous mansion on top of North Hill that his father had constructed for his first wife. Even seventy-five years later, he could smell the pungent odor of his father's shaving soap; feel the steam rising from the washbasin as his father enjoyed his morning shaving ritual.

Could this actually *be* his father's case?

But no. His father's razor case had been adorned with a gold medallion set into the center of the lid, a medallion that was engraved with the same two ornately intertwined C's with which everything Charles Connally owned had been monogrammed.

On this case there was only a simple ivory medallion.

Yet he was certain he'd seen it before.

Lifting the lid to expose a blue velvet lining, he gazed for a moment at the tortoiseshell handle of the straight razor that lay within, then picked the instrument up and opened its blade.

For just a second he didn't understand what the brown stains on the gleaming metal were. But then, as he saw the two M's etched into the tortoiseshell of the handle, he knew, in a rush of understanding that came at him like a gale force wind, exactly where he'd seen this case before.

It had belonged to his brother-in-law, Malcolm Metcalf. It had been a wedding gift from Harvey's sister, Olivia. Harvey himself had helped Olivia select it for her fiancé.

As he stared at the brown stains on the razor's blade, Harvey slowly understood their origin too.

Blood.

The blood of his niece, Mallory Metcalf?

Was it possible that after all these years, he was holding in his hands the long-missing instrument of Oliver's sister's death?

Why had it been delivered to him?

What was he being told?

And by whom?

For a long time Harvey Connally sat at his desk, the razor clasped in his suddenly palsied fingers. Over and over again he reviewed the pieces of the puzzle that he had gathered in his mind during the past weeks. Over and over again, the only face that emerged from the mists of the past was that of Malcolm Metcalf.

But he knew that wasn't quite true, for on the day that

Mallory had died—on the day that the razor Harvey was now holding had slashed across her throat and ended her life—there had been another person present.

A person for whom this instrument—this gift from the past—might hold far more meaning than it did even for him.

Laying the razor gently back in its case and snapping shut the mahogany lid, Harvey Connally came to a decision.

And picked up the telephone.

Chapter 4

*I*t *was a day in mid-March—not the worst of weather, but far from the best. Though for the last few days it seemed as if the harsh winds of winter had finally died away, they reappeared this morning, whipping out of the northeast with a chill that threatened to freeze the buds on the still-bare trees before they had a chance to open. The few tiny crocuses that had dared to poke their heads up so early in the year cowered in the cold as though trying to retreat into the safety of the scarcely thawed earth. Harvey Connally was getting ready to drive up to Manchester for a board meeting—it seemed there were more board meetings to attend every month—though he was sorely tempted to plead illness, build a fire in his library, and curl up with his worn copy of* Billy Budd, *to Harvey's mind a far superior work to the more celebrated but nearly unreadable* Moby-Dick. *Harvey Connally, however, was not the sort to follow the tide of popular opinion. He had been brought up with a sense of duty as solid as the granite beneath the soil of New Hampshire, and even as temptation whispered to him, he knew he would turn away from its siren call.*

Billy Budd would simply have to wait, perhaps even until next winter.

He was just about to leave the house when the extension telephone he'd had installed in the kitchen—a luxury to which he had quickly become accustomed—rang shrilly, with a tone that set off an alarm in Harvey's mind. Though his keenly honed rationality told him it was impossible for that bell to have a different ring in an emergency than under normal circumstances, he nevertheless felt a faint foreboding as he picked the receiver off the hook and held it to his ear.

"Harvey? Is that you?"

Harvey Connally recognized the voice coming through the line instantly, though it was far louder than usual, and quavering badly. As badly, in fact, as it had quavered the night four years ago when it informed him of the death of his sister.

"I'm here, Malcolm," he replied, nothing in his voice betraying the knot of apprehension that had already clutched his belly.

"I need you, Harvey. I need you to come to my office right away."

Harvey Connally did not ask why Malcolm Metcalf needed to see him at that very minute, for there were things—many things—one simply did not discuss on the telephone. His brother-in-law's strained urgency told Harvey that this was one of those things. "I'll be there in five minutes," he said. Without another word, he pressed the telephone's hook with his forefinger as he glanced at his watch. Dialing the operator, he asked for a number in Manchester, explained that he was unavoidably detained in Blackstone, and promised to make it to the board meeting if it proved at all possible. The man he was talking to—his roommate at Dartmouth twenty-odd years ago—asked no questions, knowing that only the most dire emergency could prevent Harvey Connally from keeping a commitment. His calendar cleared, Harvey left his house through the kitchen door, got into the DeSoto he'd purchased three weeks before, backed out of his driveway, drove along Elm Street to Amherst, turned left, and started up the hill toward the Asylum.

Harvey Connally hated the Asylum.

He hated every part of it, and always had.

Hated the building, although his own father had built it.

Certainly, he hated what went on there, convinced in his own mind that there had to be better ways to treat the mentally ill than by the use of the therapies dispensed within the blackened stone walls of the building that had become his brother-in-law's domain.

Most of all, Harvey Connally hated his brother-in-law, though nothing in his demeanor, actions, or words had ever betrayed the true depth of his feelings. Indeed, the only words he had ever spoken that might have revealed how he felt were said to his sister shortly before she married Malcolm Metcalf.

"I just want to be sure you've thought this through and are certain he's the right man for you," Harvey had told Olivia the morning after she and Malcolm announced their engagement. When Olivia assured him that she'd thought about it very carefully and was deeply in love with Malcolm Metcalf, Harvey considered the matter closed. He had not resigned his position on the Board of Trustees of the Asylum—an action that would have revealed his feelings—but as a trustee, he had removed himself from discussion of any matter relating directly to the director of the Asylum on the grounds of a conflict of interest between his roles as trustee and as the director's brother-in-law. Even after Olivia's death, Harvey had kept his feelings to himself, and Malcolm Metcalf, despite his reputation not only as a psychiatrist but as a perceptive, sensitive, and intuitive human being, had no clue that Harvey Connally hated him.

Which was exactly as Harvey Connally intended it.

As he parked the DeSoto in front of the Asylum, Harvey gazed up at the hideous facade and tried yet again to understand his father's motives in having built this immense edifice. Far larger than any other house ever built in Blackstone, the construction of this building had been an act of ostentation previously unknown in Blackstone, and totally out of character for Charles Connally. That he had turned it into a hospital for the mentally ill only a few years after having built it was just as out of character, and though Harvey Connally had spent a good deal of time searching for clues as to his father's motivations for both those peculiar actions, he'd never found answers to any of his questions.

Unconsciously taking a deep breath as he pulled the heavy front door open, Harvey stepped into the gloomy foyer, and wondered—not for the first time—how anyone could be expected to recover from an illness, mental or physical, within these cold, forbidding confines. He passed through the waiting room, and avoided looking directly at the group who huddled there—three shame-faced, obviously embarrassed people whose eyes were averted from his. The action told Harvey more than he wanted to know: they were either about to commit one of their relatives to his brother-in-law's care, or already had.

He made his way to Malcolm Metcalf's office. The latest of the director's secretaries—they never seemed to last more than a few months, and Harvey had long since *given up trying to remember their names—waved him directly into the room.*

His brother-in-law was pacing the floor, his face ashen.

"What is it, Malcolm?" Harvey Connally asked. "What's happened?"

Malcolm Metcalf's mouth worked for a moment, and finally he managed to stammer a word or two. "Mallory . . ." he said. "Oliver—"

Harvey glanced around the room, but saw no sign of either his niece or his nephew. Then he saw Malcolm Metcalf's eyes flick toward the bathroom that adjoined his office. Frowning, Harvey went to the door and pulled it open.

Red.

There was red everywhere.

It was smeared on the white-painted walls, and on the tiled floor.

There was a towel, also stained bright red, lying in a sodden heap next to the sink.

A movement, so faint he almost missed it, caught Harvey's attention, and he turned to see his four-year-old nephew cowering in a corner, his face as white as his father's and streaked with tears, his arms wrapped around his knees.

His thin form was naked, and his pale skin was also streaked with red.

And then, for the first time, Harvey Metcalf saw the bathtub.

Huge, sitting on four claw-foot legs, it was filled nearly to the rim, the water a ghastly pink.

Submerged in the bloody water, also naked, facedown, was a body.

Oliver's twin sister, Mallory.

His reason abandoning him, Harvey Connally followed the instincts that took him in two great strides from the door to the tub, where he leaned down and, plunging his arms into the gruesome liquid, lifted his niece from the water. Laying her on the floor, he turned her over to begin artificial respiration, then froze in horror.

More than a wound, the slash extended from one ear almost to the other. The child's throat had been laid open in a gash that had almost separated her head from her torso.

Harvey Connally's gorge rose in a hot flood that threatened to choke him as he stared at his dead niece, and a terrible vision flashed before him.

It was a vision of Mallory—heart-faced like her mother, with soft blond curls framing her gentle features. But instead of laughing as she so often had, her mouth was open in a dreadful, silent scream, and her eyes were wide with terror.

And from the dark, gaping wound in her throat, blood gushed in great crimson gouts as her heart quickly pumped her life away.

Onto the walls.

Onto the floor.

Into the water in which she'd been bathing.

The vision, mercifully, vanished as quickly as it had come, and Harvey Connally, knowing it was far too late to do anything for his niece, scooped his nephew from the corner. As Oliver sobbed and shook in his arms, Harvey returned to the office where his brother-in-law still stood bracing himself against the wall.

"What happened?" Harvey demanded, his voice low, almost dangerous. "Tell me what happened."

"Accident," Malcolm gasped, barely able to speak. "It was—"

"An accident?" Harvey Connally repeated. "For God's sake, Malcolm, how could you—"

Malcolm Metcalf's mouth worked spasmodically for another moment before he was able to produce any other words. Then: "Oliver," he whispered. "It wasn't me, Harvey. It was Oliver."

Harvey Connally's eyes narrowed. "How?" he demanded. "Tell me how!"

Still holding his shivering, sobbing nephew, Harvey listened as Malcolm Metcalf brokenly described what he had seen.

"They were in the tub. They loved to take baths together. And I was in here. And then I heard something. A sound—oh, God, Harvey, you can't imagine it. It was like—I don't know—a gurgling, like water going down a drain. I called to them, but—" He fell silent for a moment, then went on. "I went to the door to see what was going on. And I saw her! Oh, Lord, Harvey, I saw her die. She was in the water, and her neck was cut, and she was bleeding." Malcolm Metcalf was sobbing now, choking on his words as he struggled to get them out. "She was hanging on to the edge of the tub. I tried to help her, tried to stop the bleeding with a towel. But it was too late. She was already dying, and . . ." His words trailed off.

"And what about Oliver?" Harvey Connally asked. "Where was he?"

Malcolm Metcalf hesitated, as if wishing he didn't have to speak the words. But finally, reluctantly, they came: "Gone," he whispered. "When I realized there wasn't anything I could do for Mallory, I looked for Oliver. He—He'd gone down my private stairs, the ones that used to be the service stairs, and I found him."

"Where was he?" Harvey asked. Almost protectively, he held his nephew tighter.

There was a long silence, then Malcolm Metcalf finally spoke again. "Hiding," he said so softly that Harvey could barely hear him. "He was in one of the treatment rooms downstairs." He paused again, then: "My razor's missing," he went on, his voice dull. "I suppose Oliver must have been playing with it, and he and Mallory must have gotten into a tussle." He shook his head, his eyes welling with tears. "It was an accident," he said. "I can't believe it could have been anything else! But Oliver was so scared, he ran away and hid the razor. You can't blame him. He—He's just a little boy, Harvey. It was an accident."

For a long time Harvey Connally gazed into his brother-in-law's eyes. Then he slowly lowered his nephew to the floor and knelt down so his face was level with the little boy's. "Is that true, Oliver?" he asked. "Is what your father said true?"

Oliver Metcalf, his eyes huge, his face ashen, his whole body shaking with terror, gazed into his uncle's face.

Chapter 5

Oliver pushed open the gate in front of his uncle's house and brushed past the overgrown laurel hedge. Unless something was done this year, its branches would soon block the entrance. Not, Oliver was sure, that his uncle really cared if the gate became impassable. More and more, Harvey Connally had retreated from the life of the town, content, it seemed, to be by himself in the company of his memories. It seemed to Oliver that over the past few months, his uncle had withdrawn nearly completely from the community in which he'd lived his entire life. Oliver was uncertain as to whether Harvey Connally's self-imposed isolation was a natural result of his advancing years or a reaction to the series of tragedies that had befallen the town. The truth, he thought as he climbed the steps of his uncle's front porch, lay somewhere in between.

Not bothering to ring the bell, Oliver tried the door and discovered that it was, as always, unlocked. "Locks were invented to keep honest people out," Harvey had instructed him years ago. "They don't do a damn thing to prevent dishonest people from getting in." It was a maxim few people followed anymore; and in Blackstone, given the events of the past few months, it was a rare door indeed that was left unsecured for more than a moment or two, despite the utter lack of evidence that there was anything more than coincidence to the plague of death that had spread through the town. What had once seemed the quirky opinion of an old man trying to preserve old-fashioned ways now had the ring of prescient wisdom, Oliver thought as he stepped into the hall: none of Blackstone's locks had yet kept anyone safe.

"Uncle Harvey?" Oliver called out as he closed the door behind him. Silence. He opened his mouth to call out again, but even as he was forming his uncle's name, a cold chill of foreboding stopped him.

Something in the house was not right. He was about to start toward the kitchen, where his uncle habitually sat while he sipped his two cups of coffee and read the paper, when the old hall clock began striking the hour of ten. By this time, Harvey Connally would have finished his coffee and been at his desk, tending to the business of an elderly man: his stock portfolio and his correspondence.

Instead of turning into the dining room, Oliver moved past the base of the staircase to his uncle's study. The door was open. Harvey Connally was sitting rigidly in the leather chair behind the desk, his face ashen, his lips stretched into a tight rictus of pain.

Oliver gasped. "Uncle Harvey? What is it? What's wrong?" He moved quickly toward his uncle, his hand instinctively reaching for the telephone to summon help. Before he could lift the receiver, his uncle reached out and laid his right hand on the instrument, holding it firmly in its place.

"Not yet," he said. His voice was strained, and Oliver could see the old man's fingers trembling even as they held the receiver on its cradle. He was obviously in a great deal of pain, yet there was something in his voice that made Oliver abandon the idea of taking the telephone forcibly from his uncle's grasp. As Oliver's hands dropped to his sides, his uncle's eyes, as clear and sharp as ever, despite the old man's age and obvious pain, fixed on his. "Something was left for me this morning," he said. His lips twisted into a grimace that was intended to be a smile. "I'm not sure what it means, but I have a feeling it wasn't meant for me at all. I think it was probably meant for you." His hand moved from the telephone to the polished mahogany box that still lay on his desktop. As Oliver automatically reached for it, Harvey Connally shook his head slightly and left his hand where it was, preventing Oliver from taking the box, just as a moment ago he'd prevented his nephew from lifting the telephone. "Not yet," he said softly. Then he nodded to the chair opposite him. "Sit for a moment, Oliver."

Oliver made no move toward the chair. "Uncle Harvey, you have to let me call Dr. Margolis. You look like you're about to—" He abruptly cut off his words, but his uncle managed another smile. The piercing gaze did not waver.

"About to die?" he asked. "I think that's exactly what I'm about to do, and if you do anything—anything at all—to keep me from it, I shall do everything in my power to make your life as miserable as possible for however much longer I live. I'm old, and I'm tired; I don't mind dying. But before I go, I need to tell you something."

Slowly, reluctantly, Oliver sank into the chair across from his uncle. The old man's gaze remained fixed on him, and Oliver had an eerie feeling that his uncle was peering inside him, right to the depths of his soul.

Finally, apparently satisfied by whatever he'd seen, Harvey spoke once more.

"I have always tried to do my best by you, Oliver," he said. "I'm afraid I was not always successful, but I want you to know that I did my best, and that I never believed what your father told me. Never." He fell silent for a moment, and cocked his head as if listening to words that were coming from a distant country, a place deep in the past. Then he shook his head and spoke again. "You were never a bad boy, Oliver. You were always as good as you knew how to be." He paused, and now his eyes drifted to the mahogany box. "After I'm gone, you're going to have to deal with what is in this box. I won't try to tell you how to deal with it. You might choose simply to put it away somewhere. If you do, I advise you to put it where it cannot possibly ever again be found. If you choose to deal with it by opening the box, then I want you to keep one thing in mind."

Once again Harvey Connally's eyes fixed on Oliver's, but this time they burned with an intensity greater than Oliver had ever seen before.

"I raised you to be a Connally, Oliver," the old man said. "After your father died, and you were all I had left, I did my best to raise you as my own son." He paused again, and Oliver could see him searching for the exact words he wanted to say. Then, wincing against the pain in his chest, he made his pronouncement: "It's not your name that matters, Oliver. It's what you are inside that counts. And deep inside, Oliver, I know you are not a Metcalf. You are a Connally. You may be of his issue, but you are not your father's son!"

Suddenly, Harvey Connally's head snapped back and his eyes opened wide in an expression of surprise.

Clutching his chest, he slumped in his chair as Oliver rose to his feet and gathered his uncle into an embrace.

"No, Uncle Harvey," he begged. "Don't die! Please. You're going to be all right. I'll—"

Harvey Connally's right hand closed on his nephew's arm. "Remember, Oliver. A Connally! Always remember that I raised you to be a Connally!" His fingers tightened on Oliver's arm, sinking deep into the younger man's flesh, and then, with a deep gasp, he exhaled his last breath and his head sank down, his chin resting on his chest. As life slipped away from Harvey Connally, his grip on Oliver's arm slowly relaxed and his hand fell away. For long seconds Oliver stood still, gazing at his uncle.

Even in death, Harvey Connally's face retained its strength of character. Oliver studied that craggy, once handsome face—the face of the man who had been his only relative, his sole source of unconditional affection since the age of seven.

Always remember that I raised you to be a Connally!

Reaching down, Oliver gently closed his uncle's blue eyes, the light inside them having finally faded. As he straightened, his glance fell on the mahogany box that still sat on his uncle's desk. His first instinct was to open it and see what was inside, but even as he reached toward it, his uncle's words echoed in his memory:

You might choose simply to put it away somewhere. If you do, I advise you to put it where it cannot possibly ever again be found. . . .

Oliver's hand hovered over the box, then moved toward the telephone. Lifting the receiver from the hook, he dialed Philip Margolis's private number. The doctor picked up the phone on the third ring. "It's Oliver, Phil," he said to Margolis. "My uncle has died. I'd appreciate it if you could come over. I'm at his house."

Chapter 6

Silence at last hung over Harvey Connally's house on Elm Street. For the last two hours, as first Philip Margolis and then Steve Driver arrived, the rooms had rung with the comings and goings that attended the business of death. After Dr. Margolis's preliminary examination of the body, Harvey Connally's remains had been carried out of the house, to be transported not to Broder's Funeral Parlor but to Blackstone Memorial, where an autopsy would be performed.

"It's not really a legal necessity," the doctor had explained to Oliver, "but given recent events, I think you ought to let me do it. If I can say I did a thorough autopsy, and the cause of your uncle's death was the massive heart attack it obviously appears to be, then that should put an end to any talk." With a smile and shrug, he added, "Or at least keep it down to a dull roar, since there won't be any way to shut Edna Burnham up short of a restraining order."

Oliver managed a faint smile that conveyed his resignation in the face of the inevitable rumormongering the old lady would shortly be embarking on. "Somehow I don't think even a court order would stop Edna from . . ." His voice trailed off, but he didn't have to say any more. Even without Edna Burnham fueling the fire, there was bound to be speculation that there was more to Harvey Connally's sudden death than appeared on the surface. That assumption had already been borne out by the crowd that had begun to assemble within minutes after Steve Driver's arrival. Though no one inside the house was aware of the neighbors and passersby beyond the laurel hedge when Jeff Broder had arrived to discuss the funeral arrangements with Oliver, Broder reported that at least a dozen people were gathered on the sidewalk outside the gate. While the funeral director, whose family had been burying the dead of Blackstone for three generations, calmly went over the arrangements that Harvey Connally had made for himself several years earlier, Steve Driver went outside to try to clear the onlookers away.

He'd had no success.

Now, however, with Oliver's uncle's body gone, it seemed to Oliver as if the lodestone had been removed. By the time the last of those who had legitimate business at the house had left, the crowd too began to fall away. Their curiosity had been satisfied: they'd watched in somber silence as Harvey Connally left his house for the last time.

Oliver closed the front door after seeing Jeff Broder out. Left in the quiet of the house, he felt more alone than ever before in his life.

He began wandering slowly through the deserted rooms, acutely aware of the absence of his uncle.

After his father died, this house had been his home, at least during the times when he wasn't away, first at boarding school or at summer camp, then at college. Every room contained memories. The kitchen, where he'd sat on a stool watching his uncle's housekeeper, old

Mrs. Perry, stir the pots from which magical aromas wafted into his nostrils. The dining room, where he and his uncle had sat eating the meals Mrs. Perry fixed, and talking over anything that came into Oliver's mind. In the living room, the melodies Harvey Connally had picked out on the grand piano seemed still to hang in the air, and upstairs, in the room that had been Oliver's, he could still summon the smell of a blossom-laden summer breeze drifting in through the open window as he lay in his boyhood bed. Now, of course, the room was tinged with mustiness, the scent of disuse and abandonment, for after Mrs. Perry died, his uncle decided to look after himself, pleading that he was far too old to accustom himself to a stranger in his house.

Finally, after Oliver had wandered restlessly through every other room in the house, he could no longer put off returning to the study, where the flat mahogany box still sat on the bookshelf where he'd put it after calling Phil Margolis.

He hadn't mentioned the box to either the doctor or Steve Driver. The presence of yet another mysterious package would only become new grist for the gossip mill that was already grinding at full speed in Blackstone.

Nor had he yet opened it.

Now, as he touched its smooth surface, a strange shock ran through him, as if the case had been charged with electricity.

Had it happened before, when he'd picked up the box to move it from the desk to the bookshelf? He couldn't recall. His uncle's ominous words, swiftly followed by his sudden passing, had made the rest of the morning a blur for Oliver.

I never believed what your father told me. Never. The statement still echoed through Oliver's head.

A moment later the strange sensation passed. He picked up the box, moved back to his uncle's desk, and set it down.

As he gazed at it, he realized that it looked vaguely familiar. Examining it more closely, seeing the ornately worked medallion that was inlaid in the lid, he suddenly knew why it seemed familiar.

His father's.

It had been his father's.

But what could be in it?

He reached for it again, this time to open it, but just as his fingers touched the latches that secured the box's lid, something stopped him.

Not here!

The voice was so distinct that Oliver, startled, found himself glancing around the room to see who had uttered the words. But the room, like the house itself, was empty save for him.

Home. Take the box home.

Again the words were so clear that it was hard for Oliver to believe they'd risen from his own mind. Nonetheless, he found himself obeying them. Picking up the box, he left his uncle's house. But instead of leaving by the front door, he went out through the kitchen, down the driveway, then turned onto Harvard Street. The box, which for some reason he didn't quite understand he'd slipped under his jacket, felt almost warm, its heat penetrating his thin shirt to his skin, though he knew the warmth could be nothing more than an illusion. Quickening his step, he strode up the hill, but as he came to the burned-out wreckage of Martha Ward's house, he stopped.

Again, there was the strange sensation—almost a vibration coursing through him.

Standing stock-still, Oliver gazed at the charred remains of the house from which Rebecca Morrison had fled only a few short weeks ago. In his mind's eye, but so vividly he could have been watching the fire itself, he once more saw the flames consuming it.

Suddenly, the sound of laughter penetrated his reverie. He spun around to see who was there.

The street and sidewalk were empty.

His heartbeat speeding, Oliver continued on his way up the hill, passing the Hartwicks' but neither stopping nor even glancing at it. At the path that would lead him through the woods to the Asylum's grounds, he left the sidewalk and, out of sight of Jules and Madeline's house, felt his pulse begin to slow. Then the odd vibrating sensation vanished so abruptly and completely that he wondered whether he'd actually felt it or whether the disconcerting tingling had been nothing more than a result of the shock of his uncle's death.

Just as he emerged from the trees onto the weed-choked grounds surrounding the Asylum's hulking mass, it began again.

A heat radiating from the mahogany case. Hotter now, pulsing.

Drop it, he told himself.

Just let go of it, drop it, and walk away.

Or better yet, smash it underfoot and scatter the pieces—and whatever might be inside the box—across the field so they'd be plowed beneath the earth when the Blackstone Center project finally got under way.

Bury it under concrete. *Put it where it cannot possibly ever again be found.*

But instead of dropping the box, Oliver realized he was clutching it tighter, pressing it against his body as if at any second someone might try to snatch it from him.

He began walking again, picking his way across the grounds, but it was not toward his house that he was moving.

Instead, he drew closer and closer to the Asylum itself. With every step he took, his pulse quickened, until he could hear the sound of his own heart pounding in his ears.

He came at last to the front steps. He hesitated there, waiting for the familiar pain in his head to begin, quickly building until either he turned and fled to the sanctuary of his house or the blackness closed around him, felling him as surely as a blow to the back of the head.

Today, though, the pain did not come. Unable to stop himself, carried forward on a wave of foreboding and fear, he mounted the stone steps and reached out to grip the great latch on the door.

He paused then, and though his hand remained on the cold bronze latch, he gazed around as if taking a last look at a landscape he might never see again. He looked down the hill at the house he'd lived in for the first seven years of his life, and the last twenty-five.

For a moment—just a moment—Oliver thought he glimpsed a face in one of its windows, and he felt his heart quicken with anticipation until he realized it was nothing more than a trick of the light.

Then, out of the corner of his eye, he saw a flicker of movement. He whirled around, and as he turned, thought he saw a small figure disappearing into the woods.

A girl. A little girl, who looked like—

Mallory?

Impossible. An illusion. It had to be no more than an illusion, just as the face in the window of his house had been a fleeting and cruel illusion, and not Rebecca at all.

Yet from somewhere—somewhere distant—he thought he could barely hear a child's voice, his sister's voice, calling out to him.

Calling for him to come to her?

Or calling a warning to him, to stay away?

A trick of the light, and now a trick of the wind? A whisper, and now, nothing but silence.

His hand tightening on the latch to the Asylum's door, Oliver turned the knob and swung the heavy oak portal open.

Motes of dust hung thickly in the air inside, and the chill of the building's interior seemed to reach out and draw him in.

Steeling himself against the whipping pain he still anticipated would lash through his head at any moment, Oliver moved through the shadowy interior of the building as if in a dream, not certain where he was going, or why, but knowing he would recognize his destination when he came to it.

His footsteps echoed in the emptiness of the building, but he was hardly aware of them, for his ears were filled with other sounds.

Ghostly sounds, out of the past.

Voices whispering, mumbling incoherently.

Terrified shrieks, floating from the floors above.

Hopeless moans, seeping up from beneath the floor, surrounding him.

Oliver moved from one room to another, until at last

he came to the room that had been his father's office. There he finally took the mahogany box from beneath his jacket, and set it gently on the floor.

With trembling fingers he loosened the latches, then raised the lid.

Oliver Metcalf gazed upon the razor, and an image rose unbidden—unwanted—from the deepest realms of his subconscious.

It was a vision of the razor's blade, gleaming so bright a silver that it nearly blinded him as it arced in the air— slicing through his sister's throat.

His hands shaking, Oliver picked up the razor and opened it.

And heard his sister's dying scream . . .

Rebecca lay inside a swirling cloud of fog, a mist that engulfed her but, strangely, did not make her feel afraid, for out of the mists was emerging an image that had appeared in her dreams and fantasies for as long as she could remember. A knight, his armor burnished to the finish of a mirror, astride a great horse. A horse as black as coal, with a flowing mane and tail that whipped in the wind as the stallion bore the knight toward her, his banner—a streaming scarlet flag woven of the finest silk—billowing in the breeze with the softness of a cloud.

Now, far in the distance, muffled by the eddying mists, she thought she could hear the horse's hooves, and a thrill of excitement ran through her as she waited for the knight to be revealed to her. His strong face. His kind eyes.

Oliver.

It would be Oliver, riding to her rescue, racing toward her through the misty twilight to lift her up and swing her onto the steed's mighty back, where she would slip her arms around him and cling to him as they sped away.

But then, as the sound of hoofbeats grew nearer, she felt the first faint stirring of apprehension.

Abruptly, the fog closed in. She could feel the danger lurking everywhere around her, hidden just beyond the limits of her vision, waiting for the fog to thicken and the twilight to turn into night before creeping close, circling her, preparing to strike.

Ghostly faces appeared.

Eyes, feral and glinting with the fire of evil.

Snouts, tapering to cruel points.

Fangs, dripping with yellow saliva.

More eyes, yellow, and sunk deep beneath coarse brows, fixing on her with a glare of hatred.

Demons in search of souls to consume.

She tried to scream, but her throat constricted. Deafening shrieks of clattering laughter beat at her ears as if a pack of hyenas was closing on its prey, attacking, tearing it to shreds.

Rebecca turned to flee, to run from the hellhounds that drew closer with every passing second.

She twisted, turning first one way and then the other. No escape, no place to run.

The terror that had been escalating inside her erupted into panic. She threw herself hard to one side. A sharp pain shot through her shoulder, and a muffled screech of agony filled her throat, causing her to gag. Her breath caught in her lungs with a terrible, wracking heaving that convulsed her whole body—and brought her abruptly out of the clutches of the nightmare. But she awakened into the numbing fear that had held her for what seemed to be an eternity.

She became aware again of the tape that covered her eyes and mouth, blinding her and imprisoning the hacking coughs that continued to convulse her lungs until she thought her chest might actually explode.

Now, fully awake, she felt once more the aching cold that had slowly taken possession of every cell in her body, and for a moment she almost wished she could retreat into the fog of her dream. But then, as the fearsome, leering faces she'd seen in the mists rose before her once again, she knew that sleep—and the terrors it would bring—could no longer protect her from the horror to which she had fallen victim. Banishing the visions from her subconscious, Rebecca slowly regained control over her weakening body. The queasiness in her stomach began to ease, and the tightness in her chest to loosen. Her shoulder, which she'd smashed against the hard, cold surface next to her when she'd tried to thrash her way out of the grip of the nightmare, was throbbing painfully, but she knew that with time even that ache would slowly fade.

Unless, of course, she died.

It was going to happen; she knew that now. Sooner or later, she would succumb to something that was finally too much for her to bear. Silently, lying still in the darkness, she prayed that her body would fail her first, for she had already glimpsed the terrors she would face if it was her mind that finally betrayed her. Hell could hold no horrors worse than to be submerged forever in the dreams that tormented her, or the cold, dark prison in which she lived.

Then, so slowly she was barely aware it was happening, her racing pulse at last began to slow, and one by one she began to put her terrors aside.

She was not dead yet, nor had she lost her mind.

Somewhere, she told herself, beyond the blackness and the bonds that held her, Oliver was still searching for her, would still come to rescue her from the eternal night into which she'd vanished. But even as she clung to that sweet thought, she heard once more the echoing hooves of her nightmare, and for an instant thought that perhaps her mind had failed her after all.

Not the beat of hooves sounding in the darkness.

Footsteps.

The Tormentor was drawing close.

To feed her?

To slake her thirst?

Or to offer her up to some new terror she would not be able to anticipate until it was actually upon her?

Click.

She heard the latch of the door release, then the creak of unoiled hinges.

The sound of leather soles on a hard floor.

She sensed him now, standing above her.

Could he see her?

Did he know who she was?

Did he even care?

Or was she only someone who had come to hand? As she'd run through the darkness of that night that was now nearly lost in the dim recesses of her memory, fleeing the Wagners' in hope of getting help, had her abductor found her by accident?

Rebecca held herself perfectly still, and uttered no

sound at all, determined to let him know nothing of her fear or her pain.

If he sensed her weakness, surely he would kill her.

The dark figure gazed down upon his prize. Everything was almost right, everything in readiness.

Yet not quite.

Things were not exactly as they had been, not precisely as he saw them in his mind's eye.

He reached down and turned a tap.

The tub in which his prisoner lay slowly began to fill.

Then he turned away, having no need to watch until the climactic moment came.

The moment for which he'd waited, had prepared for so many years ago, and that now had finally arrived.

But not yet.

Not quite yet.

Not until the tub was filled.

And every memory savored.

For a moment, when she heard the trickle of water from a tap, Rebecca felt a flash of hope—he'd come to give her water.

But then, when no fingers tore the tape from her mouth or held a glass to her lips, she realized that it was something else.

And when she felt the icy water touch her legs, felt the freeze of winter truly begin to numb her flesh, she realized what her fate was going to be.

She understood the cold smoothness of the surface her face had touched, grasped the meaning of the hardness of everything around her. She was lying in a tub, and the Tormentor was filling it with water.

He was going to drown her.

Unless, before she drowned, the chill of the near-frozen water killed her first.

She felt the courage and determination she'd mustered only a few moments ago drain away, and knew, at long last, that the end was near.

Chapter 7

Oliver stared at the razor in his hand. Everything around it was lost in darkness. He could see nothing but the razor's glistening blade and, on its bright steel surface, the blood. The blood glimmering in the dark, slick and fresh, scarlet and thick. As he stared at it, it seemed to come alive, flowing across the blade toward thc fingers that clutched the razor's handle.

His fingers.

Yet, strangely, not his fingers.

Then he heard a voice: "Daddy? Daddy, I don't want to! I want to go outside!"

The voice echoed in Oliver's head. A frightened, small voice. A stranger's voice, yet not unfamiliar.

"Please?" the voice begged. "Please can't I go outside?"

The voice sounded more familiar now, and a shiver of fear crept down his back, but still he couldn't quite place it.

Then another voice spoke, with a timbre that was hard and unyielding and instantly recognizable, though he hadn't heard it in nearly forty years. "You're a bad boy," the voice said. "You're a very bad boy, and you'll do as I say!"

Oliver's fear congealed into a terror that crawled up

from his subconscious like a demon from Hell, reaching out to grasp him in its sharp-clawed fingers. His father's voice.

"Tell me what you did, Oliver."

Oliver tried to shrink away into the darkness—shrink from the voice, cower away from the demon inside that was quickly taking possession of him, draining his strength, twisting his reason, threatening to destroy his mind. But there was no escape, no place to hide, neither from his father's voice nor from the terror within.

"Tell me, Oliver," his father's voice commanded again. "Tell me what you are. Tell me what you did."

"I'm a bad boy," the little boy's voice said again, and now Oliver recognized it clearly.

His voice.

He was hearing his own voice.

"I'm a very bad boy."

"That's right," his father's voice replied. "You're a very, very bad boy."

The darkness around the gleaming razor began to fade to the silvery gray of dawn, and slowly the razor and its glistening coat of blood began to fall from focus. But the light kept brightening, until finally Oliver had to squeeze his eyes closed against it. Then he heard his father's voice once more, and knew he was powerless to disobey.

"Open your eyes, Oliver," Malcolm Metcalf's voice commanded. "Open them."

Oliver is standing just inside the front door to the Asylum. His father's hand is squeezing his own so tightly it hurts, but Oliver knows there is no way he can pull his hand free and run from his father into the sunshine outside.

He flinches as the huge oak door swings closed behind him with a thud that seems to echo through the great open room forever.

No one else, though, seems to hear it.

His father is moving now, taking such great long strides that Oliver, even though his stubby legs are moving as fast as he can make them, can barely keep up with him.

There are people all around him.

Some of them he recognizes. Women in white clothes. Nurses. Men in white coats. Doctors. There are others too, whose clothes look to Oliver just like the ones the doctors wear, but he knows they aren't doctors.

Until a little while ago, he hadn't known what the other ones— the ones who weren't doctors—did.

But now he knows, and when one of them says hello to him, Oliver doesn't say hello back.

There are other people too, people dressed in pajamas and bathrobes even though it isn't even close to bedtime, even for Oliver.

Finally, they come to the top of a long flight of stairs, steep stairs that descend into darkness. Oliver's heart begins to thump and it's hard for him to breathe. Down. They go down the stairs into the blackness below until they come to the bottom and his father leads him down a long hall. There are closed doors on both sides of the hall, and Oliver tries not to look at any of them, fearful of what might lie beyond.

At last, his father opens one of the doors.

"No, Daddy," Oliver whimpers. "Please, Daddy, don't make me—"

But it is too late. His father drags him through the door, then closes it behind them.

There is a sharp click as the lock slides home.

His father lets go of his hand, and Oliver, so terrified that his legs have lost their strength, falls to the floor, then scuttles back against the wall. Whimpering with fear, he watches as his father goes to a cabinet, opens its door, and takes out a long metal tube, from one end of which two shiny metal nubs stick out.

"No, Daddy," Oliver whispers. "No . . ."

As Oliver cowers against the wall, his father presses the end of the metal tube against the bare skin of Oliver's leg.

"Don't talk back to me, Oliver," Malcolm Metcalf says, his voice harsh. "Don't ever talk back to me!"

A jolt of electricity shoots through Oliver's leg. He shrieks as the muscles of his leg jerk spasmodically, and his foot strikes his father's shin.

"Don't kick," Malcolm Metcalf commands. "Don't you dare kick me!"

Again the metal tube touches Oliver, this time on the other leg, and instantly a second shock buzzes through him. His foot smashes painfully against the tiled wall, and another squeal erupts from his throat.

His father towers over him. "Be quiet! Take it like a man!"

As the terrible metal tube hovers near him, Oliver tries to scuttle away. He is crying now, partly from fear, partly from the burning sting of the prod, as his father comes after him with the metal stick.

Shock after shock jolts through him; his muscles contract spasmodically with each one until he is wailing, a high, keening cry, punctuated with screams of pain every time a shock courses through him.

"Be quiet, Oliver!" his father demands. "You must learn to do as I tell you!"

Oliver tries once more to wriggle away from his father's wrath, but there is no escaping the towering figure.

Zap!

Another shock. Another spasm.

On all fours, Oliver tries to crawl between his father's legs.

Zap!

His arms and legs splay in every direction, and he drops onto his stomach.

Zap!

He rolls over, curling into a tight ball.

Zap!

He feels a hot wetness spread from his crotch, and begins to sob.

Zap! "Stop crying, Oliver!"

Zap! "I told you to stop crying!"

Zap! Zap! Zap!

Oliver's bowels suddenly turn to liquid, and a terrible odor fills his nostrils as one more jab of the prod costs him the last of his self-control.

Sobbing, lying in his own filth, he wraps his arms around his legs and clamps his eyes shut. His whole body shakes as he waits for the next shock. It does not come. Instead there is his father's voice.

"What are you?" Malcolm Metcalf asks.

"A bad boy," Oliver whispers. "I'm a very bad boy."

Without another word, his father unlocks the door

and leaves the room. When the door closes, Oliver has just the briefest moment of hope, but then he hears the click of the lock as his father turns it from the outside.

Crying softly, the little boy remains on the floor for a few more minutes, waiting for the pain in his body to subside. Then, knowing what he must do before the door will be unlocked again, he begins cleaning up the mess on the floor, using his shirt as a towel, washing it out over and over again at the little sink that is bolted to one of the room's walls.

He is, he knows, a very bad boy indeed.

So bad that neither his father, nor anyone else, will ever love him again.

The darkness closed around him, and once again all Oliver could see in the blackness was the glimmering blade of the razor.

The razor, and the blood of his sister.

Chapter 8

*E*verything had changed.

It seemed to Oliver that he was hanging, suspended, in some netherworld that had no relationship to Blackstone, or to the life he had lived there.

It wasn't dark—not exactly—and yet he couldn't see.

He felt as if he were deaf, yet there was no sense of sound at all, no feeling of vibration in his head, or distant muffled noises that he thought he should have heard more clearly.

His sense of touch had deserted him too, and he couldn't be certain whether he was moving or standing still.

He could have been sitting, or lying down, or even curled up, his arms wrapped around his knees the way he'd liked to sleep when he was a little boy.

A little boy . . .

The thought hung with him in the void.

That's what he was: a boy. A little boy. He was no longer Oliver Metcalf, forty-five and a responsible adult, editor of the town newspaper. Somehow, he had been transported into some other world, the world of his childhood that, without knowing it, he had years ago closed off behind a curtain of blackness. But now the curtain was parting. Before him, as he waited, the gray half-light brightened.

The first thing he knew was that he was afraid.

Afraid because he'd done something wrong.

Bad! He was a bad boy! A very bad boy!

He was a bad boy, and his father was going to punish him.

And he deserved to be punished.

Oliver waited quietly in the not-quite-dark, not-quite-light. Somehow he knew that was the right thing to do. Sometimes his father didn't come for a long time, and sometimes he came right away.

But Oliver knew he must be quiet, and he must wait. Because if he was bad, more bad things would happen.

Scraps of images began to float around him, and suddenly, the light was momentarily brighter again and he was able to catch glimpses of things.

A little girl.

She had a pretty face, framed by long blond hair, and she was holding something in her hands. A doll. A doll with a pretty porcelain face and golden hair.

Suddenly, from out of the twilight silence surrounding him, Oliver heard his father's voice. But now his father wasn't speaking to him. He was speaking to the little girl. "You can't have it anymore," his father decreed. "Little boys don't play with dolls. They play with balls and bats!"

Now Oliver could hear the little girl, her sobs enveloping him the way his father's voice had a moment ago. He saw her face, saw it change, saw the blond locks fall away, heard the cries reach a crescendo then fade away, and the strange silence fell over Oliver once again, and the child's face took on the same odd grayness that was all around.

The grayness of death.

The little boy was dead.

Dead, like Oliver's sister.

And in the twilight Oliver's father was whispering. "Do you understand?" he asked. "Do you understand why he died?"

Oliver nodded, though he didn't understand at all.

"We're going to put the doll away," his father's voice whispered. "We're going to put it away in the secret place. But you're going to remember, Oliver. You're going to remember all of it."

His father's voice faded again, leaving Oliver enshrouded in the grayness where, as before, he felt as if he was hanging in a void, suspended in a world without sensations.

A world in which there was no difference between night and day, no difference between sound and silence.

No difference between life and death.

Then a point of light appeared.

"Watch the light, Oliver," his father's voice instructed, penetrating the silence from an echoing distance that was nowhere yet everywhere.

Like the twilight itself, his father's voice was simply present.

"Watch the light, Oliver," his father's voice said again. "Watch the light and see what it does."

The light reappeared, a flame now, flickering in front of Oliver's eyes.

Then the flame began to move, and now Oliver could see something else.

An arm.

An arm covered with soft skin, soft and smooth and pale. A woman's skin.

The flame moved closer and closer to the skin.

Oliver wanted to cry out, to move the flame away from the woman's skin, but the twilight held him in its thrall as tightly as if it were made with ropes and straps.

The flame licked at the skin on the arm, and then, from out of the silence, came a sound.

The roar of a dragon.

The roar sounded again, and then Oliver saw the dragon looming out of the twilight, its eyes glowing like twin rubies, its golden scales glittering even in the strange gray light. Its mouth opened, and once again it roared, a great bellow that hung in the air as a blast of fire burst from its throat.

As suddenly as it had appeared, the dragon vanished into the twilight, and all that was left was the vision of the woman's arm, the skin charred black, great chunks of it peeling off, dropping away to reveal the raw flesh beneath.

Then, from somewhere in the gray eternity around him, Oliver heard the dragon roar once more, and the flesh before his eyes burst into flame.

Now he heard his father's voice. "Do you understand, Oliver?"

"I understand," Oliver silently breathed.

"You will remember?" his father's voice demanded, and though the words were formed into a question, Oliver understood what would happen if he forgot.

"I will remember," he promised.

"We will put the dragon with the doll," his father's voice whispered. "And when next you see it, you will know to whom it should belong."

Once again time and space melded together.

Oliver hung in the gray silence.

More images flickered in front of him.

A scrap of cloth, intricately embroidered, a single letter, mirrored, worked perfectly into one of its corners.

A face appeared, and snakes writhed about him, and once again he heard his father's voice.

"Remember what I'm showing you, Oliver. Remember what I'm saying. If you forget, you know what will happen."

Oliver knew he would not forget.

And after his father had spoken, and hidden the scrap of cloth away with the doll and the dragon, those images too fell away into the gray morass, as surely as if they'd never been there at all.

"But you'll remember," his father's voice whispered. "When it's time, you will remember."

"I promise, Daddy." The words were no more than an unvoiced whimper, but they echoed in Oliver's mind as loudly as had the dragon's now-forgotten roar. "I promise . . ."

More images rose out of the gray, took focus for a moment, then disappeared so utterly that they might never have existed. And as each of them flickered through his consciousness, only to be lost again an instant later, Oliver's father's voice kept whispering.

"You'll know what to do, boy. When the time comes, you'll know what to do as surely as if you had become my own reincarnation. You are all that's left of me, and you'll do it. After they've destroyed me—after they've sent me away and destroyed my work—you will still be here. You will be my sword of vengeance. You will do exactly as I tell you, and it will be as if I'd come back myself, to destroy the destroyers.

"And do you know why you'll do it, Oliver?"

"Because I've been bad," Oliver whispered. "Because I've been a very bad boy, and I have to do whatever you want me to do."

"That's right, Oliver. You've been a bad boy." His father's words lashed out with the sting of a whip. "Killed them! Killed your mother! Killed your sister! Evil, vile child!"

Oliver tried to shrink away from the accusations, tried to find a way to drop back into the comforting silence of the twilight abyss, but there was no escape. Wherever he turned, his father's words were there, piercing into his consciousness, jabbing at him, torturing him, until finally, the last of his resistance crumpled.

"I understand, Daddy," he said. "I understand."

It was then that the darkness closed around him once again, and he sank gratefully back into an oblivion that was free not only of the strange images but of the sound of his father's voice.

It was not, though, an oblivion in which Oliver could dwell forever.

Sooner or later, consciousness would inevitably return.

Consciousness, and the evil pleasure his father demanded.

Oliver woke up in darkness.

Not the familiar darkness that blanketed his room when he woke up at night, thinking at first there was no light at all, only to find that the shadows that moved on the walls and ceiling, cast by the street lamp outside, were old friends. In that kind of darkness he could snuggle down deeper in his bed, pulling the covers up tight under his chin as he let his imagination run wild, seeing all kinds of wonderful things in the dark shapes on the walls. He liked that kind of darkness.

Some nights he imagined he was in a tent in the jungle, and the shadows he was seeing were cast by lions and tigers and elephants.

But the darkness in which he awakened this time was different.

An empty, scary kind of darkness.

The kind of darkness that made him think that things he couldn't see were watching him.

The kind of darkness that made him shiver, even though it wasn't cold.

"Daddy?" he called out, keeping his voice soft enough so that if there were any wild animals lurking in the darkness, they might not hear him.

There was no answer. As Oliver came fully awake, he realized he wasn't in his bed at all.

He wasn't even in his room.

And his whole body was sore.

The blackness turned to a funny gray color; then, as it grew brighter, became a bright, blinding white, as a powerful, naked bulb switched on.

White tiles on the floor. And on the wall.

White paint on the ceiling.

And then his father's face, looming above him, flanked by two big men in white coats.

"You're not a very good boy, Oliver," his father said. "You're a bad boy. A very bad boy, who killed his sister."

"I didn't!" Oliver cried. "I—"

Before he could finish his sentence, his father pressed a button in a wooden box. Oliver convulsed as the jolt of electricity passed through him. Then, as his body relaxed, he cried:

"No!"

His father pressed the button again. This time as the shock shuddered through him, a gush of vomit spewed from his mouth.

"Clean him," Oliver's father said, and the two men in white coats stepped over to the table and began wiping the vomit away with a towel.

His father pressed the button again. He was sobbing now, whimpering, his stomach churning, his throat filling with bile as his body reacted to the torture.

Then, in a small voice that seemed to come from somewhere outside himself, Oliver heard himself say, "I've been a bad boy. A very bad boy."

"That's right," his father said. "A very bad boy. And now I'm going to tell you why you're a bad boy, and what you did."

His breath coming in short, shallow gasps, Oliver listened as his father explained how he had taken the razor and what he had done with it. His father's voice droned on and on, and as he spoke, tears came into Oliver's eyes.

Tears of sorrow, and tears of shame.

And at last, when it was over, and he understood everything his father had told him, he slipped from the white tiled room and pulled the door closed behind him. Outside in the corridor the cries and screams that had echoed through the building for so long could still be heard, but not by Oliver Metcalf.

All he could hear as he slowly mounted the stairs

toward the first floor was the sound of his father's voice, repeating over and over what he, a very bad boy, had done. And telling him what still was left to do.

Chapter 9

Rebecca Morrison was staring at the face of Death.

She had no conscious memory of when the apparition had appeared; nor did she have any idea how long she had been gazing upon it.

It was simply there, hanging in front of her in the darkness.

It was a pale, bloodless face, almost lost in the folds of a deep hood whose black cloth blended into the surrounding darkness so perfectly that the face itself seemed almost to be a part of the blackness. Though there seemed to be no source of light, the face was limned in shadows, shadows that moved and seemed to shimmer with a life of their own.

Yet the face was dead.

Wattles of skin hung around the neck, and the jaw was slack, causing a lipless maw to gape wide, exposing the rotted teeth within. The tongue, covered with open sores, was coated with a yellowish goo that strung out to the broken teeth like strands of a spiderweb; a spiderlike creature, fat and mottled black-brown, lurked deep in the specter's throat, crawling out long enough for Rebecca to catch only a glimpse of it before scuttling back down into its fleshy lair. The creature set Rebecca's flesh crawling, with its multiple hairy legs and the grizzly morsels that hung from its curving, dripping mandibles.

Above the maw a great beaked nose curved out from a sloping brow, its grayish skin pocked deep with ulcerations. Mucous ran thickly from its nostrils. On either side of the hooked nose, glowering eyes were sunk deep in hollowed sockets. The eyes, like the rest of the specter's mien, were gray and dead, but from somewhere deep within them, a cold harsh light—a flame of evil—flicked like the tongue of a serpent.

The cigarette lighter, Rebecca thought. The present Oliver and I found for Andrea. It's as if the dragon's tongue were caught in the eyes of Death.

She tried to turn away, tried not to look at the terrible face, but something about it held her in thrall. There was a terrible hunger in the face, a yearning in the coldly flickering eyes, a depraved lust as it gazed upon her.

It's come for me, Rebecca thought. Death wants me, and has come for me.

All her senses were playing tricks on her now.

She had no idea how long it had been since the Tormentor carried her up the stairs, no idea of what it was he wanted. When he'd finally set her down, she'd found herself lying on something hard and cold. As her hands, still bound behind her back, explored the smoothly rounded surface on which she lay, it had come to her.

A bathtub.

He'd put her in a bathtub.

And then, almost at the very instant she'd realized where she was, he'd opened the valve.

Not far.

Just enough so that the water began slowly to fill the tub.

Rebecca braced herself, tried to prepare herself for

what might happen if he tore her clothes from her body. She turned her mind inward, searching within herself for something to sustain her through the ordeal she was certain was coming.

Oliver!

She would think about Oliver, and no matter what the Tormentor might do to her, it wouldn't touch her.

She wouldn't feel it.

Wouldn't respond to it.

And when it was over, it would be as if it had never happened.

As the tub had filled, she conjured a picture of Oliver in her mind, imagined him smiling at her, saw his gentle eyes watching over her, felt his hands caressing her.

Listened to his voice consoling her, encouraging her, giving her strength.

The water slowly rose in the tub, covering first her feet and then her legs. The water, still carrying the icy chill of winter, numbed every part of her body it touched. Rebecca, inured to cold, turned away from the icy wetness as completely as she had turned away from the Tormentor, utterly closing her senses to it, putting herself in a place where she neither felt nor heard anything that did not emanate from within her own mind.

In her mind she was not alone.

Oliver was with her.

Oliver was looking after her.

Until, suddenly, Oliver was no longer there, and in his place the visage of Death hung before her again.

Her senses too had come alive. She could smell the fetid breath of the specter, feel the frigid water.

Was this what Aunt Martha had seen and felt as she died?

When she'd gazed transfixed upon the face of her savior, had she too seen Death leering hungrily down on her?

Had she already died?

But no—she could still feel the hardness of the tub, the wetness of the water.

The water still ran slowly into the tub. It covered her waist in an ice-cold blanket; its tentacles were reaching up toward her chest.

In the darkness surrounding her, Rebecca saw the lipless mouth of Death twist in a grisly parody of a smile.

Then, over the sound of running water, she heard something else.

A door opened.

Footsteps approached.

The Tormentor had returned.

Oliver stood in the center of his father's office, so that the great walnut desk with the huge leather chair behind it loomed directly in front of him. His father would have to look neither to the right nor to the left to see him.

That was important.

When you were going to be punished, it was important to face it straight on. His father had told him that over and over again, but it was still hard.

So hard, in fact, that Oliver hadn't quite been able to look up. But now he heard his father's voice: "Oliver."

Biting his lower lip to keep from crying out, Oliver finally looked up.

His father's chair was empty.

He glanced almost furtively around the room, certain that his father must be there somewhere, but the sofa against the wall to the left was empty, and so was the wing-backed chair that faced his father's desk. Then his eyes fell on the portrait of his mother that hung on the wall of his father's office.

There was a black ribbon draped over its frame.

He was still gazing up at the picture when he heard his father's voice again: "Come into the bathroom, Oliver. Come and look at what you've done."

Fear forcing him to obey, Oliver moved to the door cut into the wall to the right, turned its knob, and pushed it open.

He saw nothing.

"Look," his father commanded. "Look in the mirror, and see what you've done."

Oliver moved to the sink and stared into the mirror that hung on the wall above it. But instead of seeing his own face, he found himself gazing upon the face of his father.

The face in the mirror was covered with a soapy lather, and one cheek had been scraped clean.

Then, from behind him, Oliver heard the sound of laughter.

The laughter of children.

Spinning around, he found himself once again staring at his four-year-old self.

He was in the bathtub, and his sister was with him. They sat at opposite ends of the great claw-footed tub, laughing happily as they splashed each other, then smeared each other's faces with soapy bubbles.

"Stop that," he heard his father's voice say.

In the tub, Oliver and Mallory kept splashing, kept laughing.

"I said, stop that!" His father's voice was angry now.

In the bathtub, Oliver and Mallory, caught up in their game, ignored their father's command.

Then Mallory, with a silvery peal of happy laughter, stood up in the tub and used both her little hands to heave a great splash of soapy water at her father.

The little Oliver in the tub, stunned by what his sister had done, froze, his wide and fearful eyes fixing on his father.

And Oliver Metcalf, still standing at the sink, raised his right arm. In his hand, the blade of the razor he'd brought into the Asylum less than two hours ago glinted brightly.

Rage filled Oliver as he heard his father's voice once more, trembling with cold fury as he glowered down at his little daughter. "Don't you dare laugh!" he thundered. "After what you've done, don't you dare laugh!"

But Mallory, caught up in her game, only splashed the water harder, her laughter growing louder and louder.

Suddenly, Oliver's arm flashed out, and then—

The stab of pain seared through his head, wiping out the vision he'd just seen, plunging him into the familiar abyss of darkness. But even as he felt himself sinking into unconsciousness, he heard his father's voice.

"No, Oliver! Open your eyes! Open your eyes and see what you have done!"

Slowly the blackness faded away, and the pain in Oliver's head subsided. He opened his eyes.

And found himself gazing at his sister's naked body, submerged facedown in the tub.

He was out of the tub now, and his father was putting the razor into his hand.

"Look what you've done, Oliver," his father told him. "It wasn't me, Oliver. It was you! All of it is your fault! Your fault that your mother died, Oliver! She didn't die giving birth to Mallory, Oliver! She died giving birth to *you*! And now you've killed Mallory too. Killed her, Oliver. Killed your sister!" His father's voice grew louder and louder, until the words pounded in Oliver's head, each one striking him like a blow. "Killed her, Oliver! Killed her!"

"No," Oliver whimpered. "No, Daddy, I didn't—"

"Killer!" Malcolm Metcalf roared. "Killer! *Killer! KILLER!*" His voice kept rising, and the word became a chant, then divided itself into two words: "Killer . . . killer . . . kill her! *Kill her! KILL HER!*"

Oliver reached down, grasped his sister, lifting her from the tub, turning her over to gaze into her face.

Still his father's voice roared in his head. "Kill her! Kill her!"

He raised the blade high, his hand trembling as he prepared to obey his father's order: "KILL HER!"

Rebecca tensed as she felt the touch of fingers on her flesh. But it was different this time: the cold slickness of latex was gone. Her body was being lifted out of the tub, and a second later the tape was torn from her eyes and mouth. Even the shadowy light of the bathroom blinded her for a second, but then her vision cleared and she recognized the face above her.

"Oliver!" she cried out. "Oliver!"

Then she saw the razor in his hand, the glinting blade slashing downward, and opened her mouth once more. "Oliver!"

Rebecca's scream sliced through the chaos in Oliver's mind. In an instant his father's voice fell silent. His sister's face vanished, replaced by Rebecca Morrison's sweet features. But the razor was already slashing toward her, its cutting edge ready to slice deep into her throat in obedience to his father's order.

Then, in the last instant, the blade millimeters from her neck, his arm jerked, changed course, and instead of cutting into Rebecca's flesh, the blade released her from the bonds that held her. The razor clattered to the floor. As Oliver stood, shocked into immobility by the realization of what he had nearly done, Rebecca's arms slid around his neck and she buried her face in his shoulder.

Cradling Rebecca in his arms, Oliver carried her out of the bathroom, through the empty room that had once been his father's office, and out into the corridor. A moment later he kicked the front door of the Asylum open and stepped out into the warm sunshine of the spring afternoon.

Chapter 10

Oliver set Rebecca down only long enough to open the front door to his house, then gathered her into his arms again, carried her inside, and up the stairs to the guest room. Lowering her gently onto the bed, he pulled a blanket over her. "I'll get you some towels and a robe," he said as he started toward the door.

By the time he returned, the clothing Rebecca had been wearing since the moment she'd run out of Clara and Germaine Wagner's house was lying in a heap next to the bed, and Rebecca was huddling under the covers, shivering so hard her teeth were chattering. Her skin was so pale it had taken on a bluish color, and her hair, matted, wet, and filthy, hung limply around her haggard face.

I did this, Oliver thought wretchedly. I did this to Rebecca. Dropping to his knees, he took her hand in both of his. "I'm sorry," he whispered. "Oh, God, Rebecca, I'm so sorry. I'll never—"

Rebecca frowned. "Sorry for what?" she asked. "You saved me, Oliver. You saved me from that horrible man who . . ." Her voice died away as a shudder shook her entire body at the memory of what she'd just gone through. Then, as Oliver started to speak again, she held her fingers to his lips. "Not now," she pleaded. "Please? I'm so cold, and so tired, and so hungry." Oliver choked as a sob rose to his throat, and Rebecca squeezed his hand. "Could you maybe make me some soup?" she asked. "Maybe if you could make me some soup, I could take a shower and get warmed up again, and then you can tell me all about how you found me."

Oliver felt a terrible pain in his chest—a pain that stabbed directly at his heart—and wondered if it was possible his heart could actually be physically breaking. *She doesn't understand! She doesn't understand at all!*

"Please?" Rebecca asked again. "Just not right now, Oliver."

Oliver hesitated, his mind churning, needing to make her understand the magnitude of the terrible thing he had done, but at the same time wishing there were some way he would never have to tell her at all. Even as the wish rose in his mind, he knew it was impossible. But certainly he could spare her the knowledge of what he'd done for a few more minutes. "Of course," he whispered. "I'll go find something for you. The bathroom's just through there." He started toward the door once more, but then looked back at Rebecca. "You'll be all right by yourself?" he asked anxiously.

"Of course I will," Rebecca assured him. "Besides, you'll be right downstairs. What could happen to me?"

She smiled at him then, and Oliver tried to etch that smile so deeply into his memory that he could never forget it. Once she understood what he had done, he would never see her smile again. Then he turned away and left Rebecca alone.

He found a can of chicken soup in the kitchen, opened it, and emptied its contents into a bowl, which he put in the microwave. While the soup heated, he picked up the telephone and punched Phil Margolis's number into the keypad. "It's Oliver," he said when the doctor came on the line. "I've found Rebecca." Before Margolis could ask any questions, Oliver spoke again. "She was in the Asylum. I think she's all right, but if you could come over to my house—"

"I'll be there in ten minutes," Philip Margolis broke in.

Oliver hung up, then picked the receiver up again, and this time called Steve Driver. "Steve?" he said, after explaining that Rebecca was with him. "Edna Burnham was right. It was all connected." A pause. Then: "And I know what the connection was."

There was a silence. "Is that all you're going to say?" Driver asked. "Or are you going to tell me what the connection was?"

"Me," Oliver said softly. "It was me, Steve."

Now the silence stretched out so long Oliver wondered if the deputy was still there. But then Steve Driver spoke again. "I guess I better come over."

"I guess so," Oliver said, his voice as spiritless as he suddenly felt. Hanging up the phone, he checked the soup, set the microwave to keep it warm until Rebecca came downstairs, then set a place for her at the kitchen table.

He was putting an English muffin in the toaster oven when, at almost the same moment, two cars pulled up in front of his house. After showing Philip Margolis to the room he'd given Rebecca, he led Steve Driver into the kitchen. "You want a cup of coffee or something?" His voice was as dull as it had been on the phone a few minutes earlier.

"I'd like to hear what happened," the deputy replied. "Or at least what you think happened."

Oliver cast about in his mind, trying to decide where to begin. A lot of what occurred in the Asylum that day was still jumbled in his memory. Images crowded into his mind, and he shuddered involuntarily as he remembered the scenes of his childhood suffering that had been unlocked from his memory.

"I think it started the day my sister died," he finally said.

Steve Driver, frowning, sank into one of the kitchen chairs. "That was forty years ago," he said.

Oliver nodded. "Uncle Harvey gave me something this morning, before he died." The deputy's frown deepened, but he said nothing, and Oliver continued. "It was a straight razor, in a mahogany box. He found it on his porch when he got his paper." Oliver's eyes met Steve Driver's. "It was my father's razor. My father used it to kill my sister. Then he convinced me that I did it."

Slowly, forcing himself to speak evenly and without emotion, Oliver related what had happened to him in the Asylum that day, all the memories that had come back to him. At some point, while Oliver talked, Philip Margolis joined Steve Driver at the kitchen table. The two men listened silently. Steve Driver took some notes, but never interrupted Oliver.

"That's what the headaches and the blackouts were about," Oliver explained to Margolis. "It wasn't anything physical at all. It was just too many memories that were too painful to face. And every time I went near the Asylum—every time the memories started to come to the surface—I shut them out. I gave myself headaches. I blacked out. I did everything to keep from remembering. And it was what my father wanted." He shook his head, recalling the scenes he had finally relived, the veil of blackness now forever stripped away. "All those things that started showing up the last few months?" he said. "That doll belonged to Bill McGuire's aunt. And the dragon lighter? That was Martha Ward's sister's. He showed me all those things when I was a child. And he planted it all in my mind." A bitter smile twisted his lips. "It was his revenge. *I* was his revenge. His reincarnation, he told me, all that was left of him to do his bidding. He used me to send something back to every family that ever had anything to do with that place." He fell silent for a moment, then spoke again. "It was I who kidnapped Rebecca," he said quietly. "I kidnapped her, and I tied her up in there, and I—"

"No!"

The single word was uttered with such force that all three of the men in the kitchen flinched. Then, as one, they turned to see Rebecca Morrison standing in the doorway. She was wrapped in Oliver's thick terry-cloth bathrobe, far too large for her small form, its belt sashed tightly around her waist. Her hair, clean and dry now, created a soft frame around her heart-shaped face.

Her eyes were fixed on Oliver.

"You didn't hurt me, Oliver," she said quietly. "You saved my life."

Oliver rose and took a step toward her, shaking his head. "Rebecca, you don't understand. I—"

Quickly, Rebecca crossed the kitchen and once more put her finger to Oliver's lips. "I know what you did, Oliver," she said. "I was there, remember? I was there when I was kidnapped, and I was there all the time that man held me in the Asylum. And I was there when you came for me."

"But you don't understand—" Oliver began again.

Rebecca took both his hands in her own. "I do under-stand," she said. "I understand that you love me, and I understand that I love you. And that's all there is." When Oliver tried to speak again, she shook her head, repeating, "That's all there is."

Oliver gazed into Rebecca's face for a long time, then finally tore his eyes away to look at Steve Driver and Philip Margolis. Regardless of what Rebecca had said, they must have understood the truth.

But Steve Driver was tearing his notes from his pad, and while he slid the notebook itself back into the inside pocket of his jacket, Philip Margolis spoke for both of them.

"It's her word against yours, Oliver," the doctor said. "And we all know that Rebecca doesn't lie. She just plain doesn't."

Finally, Oliver put his arms around Rebecca and pulled her close, his lips nuzzling her hair as she clung to him. But then he caught a glimpse of the Asylum looming on top of the hill outside the window. He released Rebecca from his embrace and his expression hardened. "I'll be back in a few minutes," he said. "There's something I've got to do."

Leaving the house, Oliver strode up the hill to the spot where the wrecking ball still stood, waiting for the work to proceed. Climbing into the seat in front of its controls, he found the starter switch, and the machine's engine roared to life. He studied the controls, then began working the various levers.

A moment later the enormous lead ball swung back on its cable, paused for an instant at the end of its arc, then moved again, gaining momentum as Oliver aimed it at the great stone edifice.

As the ball smashed into the wall, glass shattered and rock exploded in every direction.

Again and again Oliver sent the ball crashing against the Asylum's wall. With every blow a little more of the pain his father had inflicted on him when he was a boy was finally relieved.

The battering went on and on, until, too weak to stand any longer, the prisonlike wall of the Blackstone Asylum collapsed.

Oliver Metcalf at last was free.

Epilogue

The white clapboard Congregational church, with its high steeple and brass bell, had stood guard over Blackstone for more than two centuries. Now, as the bell began to toll the hour of four, nearly all the citizens of Blackstone left their homes and began moving slowly toward the cemetery, as if drawn by the stately, mournful gong, inexorably, like iron filings to a magnet. They came from all directions, from the "College Streets" of Harvard, Princeton, and Amherst, north of the square, and from the less grand thoroughfares that lay in a grid to the south. As ancient custom dictated, they congregated briefly in the square itself, neighbors greeting neighbors, lifelong friends chatting quietly for a few minutes before gathering into larger groups that moved west toward the white picket fence that surrounded the graveyard.

It had been three days since Harvey Connally had died; three days since Oliver Metcalf had carried Rebecca Morrison out of the Asylum.

Three days since Oliver had taken the controls of the wrecking ball and smashed the wall of the Asylum itself.

Three days in which more rumors had crept through the streets of Blackstone, moving from house to house, passed from lip to ear in whispers so quiet that the words could barely be understood. Where the tale began—which mouth first uttered the words—no one could say, for it is never possible to trace a rumor back to its first seed. But by four P.M. on this cloud-darkened afternoon, when it was finally time to lay Harvey Connally's body to rest, there was barely a soul in Blackstone who had not heard the story. A legend was taking root.

A legend about a man who, throughout his entire lifetime, the town had honored and held in great esteem.

A man who, in death, was taking on a new role, a role he would undoubtedly continue to play through the decades—perhaps even centuries—to come.

Harvey Connally, the rumor proclaimed, had been the one who delivered the gifts, and with them the curse on half a dozen of Blackstone's oldest families, including his own.

"It's crazy," Bill McGuire said when someone—he could no longer remember exactly who—had first whispered it to him. "Harvey could never have done such a thing." But by the end of the day, when he'd gone into the library to gaze upon the portrait of his aunt—her face suddenly appearing to him so similar to that of the doll with which his daughter still slept every night—he'd wondered. Bill McGuire knew little about that aunt, except that she'd been killed in a boating accident years earlier—long before he was born—after some tragedy had befallen her own child.

The details of that tragedy had never been explained to him.

Harvey Connally, though, would have known his aunt, and known what happened to her.

He could even have known if the doll had once belonged to her, or to her child.

Bill McGuire couldn't be sure, and though he still insisted that the doll had nothing to do with Elizabeth's death, doubt had been planted and was beginning to grow. Though Bill didn't want to believe the whispers about Harvey Connally, neither could he deny them outright. Today, as he moved toward the cemetery for the burial service, he found himself hoping that somehow, at this final moment before Harvey Connally was laid to rest, the truth might somehow be revealed.

Perhaps, Bill thought, he might simply *feel* something. Something that would tell him that the evil that had settled over Blackstone was finally coming to an end with Harvey Connally's interment.

Though she hadn't yet talked to Bill McGuire, Madeline Hartwick, with Celeste at her side, was attending the service in the cemetery for much the same reason as the contractor. She had heard the whispers about Harvey Connally only yesterday, when she had come back from Boston, where she was staying with Celeste in the small apartment they had found. Throughout a sleepless night, the first she had spent alone in the house in which Jules had terrorized her on the last night of his life, Madeline paced the chilly rooms of the mansion at the top of Harvard Street, returning time after time to the portrait of Jules's mother that she had hung on the library wall the fateful evening of the engagement party.

As she gazed at the portrait of Louisa Hartwick, she

clutched in her hand the locket that Celeste had found in the melting snow a few weeks after Jules died.

The locket that Madeline had finally opened, and discovered was engraved—in letters so tiny she'd needed a magnifying glass to read them—with twin monograms: LH and MM.

It hadn't taken Celeste long to guess what names the monograms stood for: Louisa Hartwick and Malcolm Metcalf. With the guess had come the knowledge of why the portrait of her husband's mother, wearing the apron of a volunteer at the Asylum, had been hidden away in the attic: her husband's mother must have had an affair with Oliver Metcalf's father.

And Harvey Connally, brother of Malcolm Metcalf's wife, must have found out.

Had he found the locket after all these years, and left it in her car that night, knowing it would send her husband into a paranoid rage?

But how could he have? Until that night, Jules had shown no signs at all of paranoia. But might Harvey Connally have known something about her husband's family that she did not? Might it not even be possible that some grudge, long forgotten by anyone except himself, might have been festering in Harvey Connally for years, and now, as his life drew to a close, he'd decided to try to even the score?

Madeline Hartwick, like Bill McGuire, had not quite been able to dismiss the words she'd heard about Harvey Connally, and though she didn't yet believe them, neither could she disbelieve them.

So she too had come to the service not only because

Harvey Connally had been a part of her life for so many years but because she was hoping for some kind of sign.

A sign that could lead her to the truth.

As the questions and rumors had passed from one set of lips to another, more and more small facts had been remembered about Harvey Connally.

One person reminded another that there were few secrets in Blackstone that Harvey Connally hadn't known; few families to whom, one way or another, he wasn't somehow related.

Hadn't he been a trustee of the Asylum, and in that capacity had he not known everything that had gone on there?

Hadn't his father *built* the Asylum, so Harvey would have known every room, every hidden passage, every dark niche?

What about Ed Becker? By the time of Harvey Connally's interment, everyone in town had been reminded that Ed's great-uncle had disappeared into the Asylum. It had been either that or spending his life in prison. Something about a girl who disappeared, wasn't it?

The stories had passed from house to house, been discussed in the Red Hen, whispered about in the library.

No one knew who first remembered hearing a rumor that years ago Martha Ward's sister had died in the Asylum, having burned herself so badly with a cigarette lighter that nothing could be done to save her.

A lighter like the one Rebecca had bought from Janice Anderson?

It wasn't long before at least three people were willing

to swear that they could now remember seeing Harvey Connally lurking near Janice's table just before Oliver and Rebecca bought the lighter Rebecca had given to her cousin Andrea. Though it had happened weeks earlier, their memories of Harvey's sinister presence there grew clearer with every telling, until no one in Blackstone questioned that the old man had been at the flea market that day.

Even the handkerchief that Oliver had given to Rebecca had been ascribed to Harvey. How many times had he been in Oliver's house? Couldn't it have been he who left the embroidered square in the attic for Oliver to find? He would have known that Oliver would give it to Rebecca. After all, didn't it have her initial worked perfectly into its intricate design?

By the third day, when the time had finally come to inter Harvey Connally's remains in the mausoleum his father had built, the tendrils of the legend had crept through Blackstone like a spreading vine, wrapping every citizen so tightly in its grip that only a few were still in doubt.

The most vocal of those was Edna Burnham.

She was the last to enter the cemetery behind the Congregational Church that afternoon, and as she came through the gate and threaded her way slowly to the corner of the graveyard in which generations of Connallys had been buried, the mourners fell silent. Edna walked steadily, her head high, and the crowd parted before her as if submitting to her silent will.

Little Megan McGuire, her left arm wrapped tightly around her doll, shrank closer to her father as the old woman paused, looking down at her with eyes that seemed to cut right through her. When the old woman reached out as if to stroke her doll's hair, Megan's mouth tightened into a deep scowl. "Don't touch her," she said, wrenching away from the old woman. "Sam doesn't like to be touched."

Edna Burnham's fingers jerked back as if they'd touched a hot iron, but then she moved on, passing Bill McGuire and Mrs. Goodrich without speaking a word.

A few steps farther on she came to Madeline Hartwick, her daughter Celeste on one side of her, Andrew Sterling on the other. Most of the employees of the bank were clustered around Andrew and the two surviving Hartwicks. Once again Edna Burnham paused, searching their faces as if looking for something, but giving no sign as to whether she had found it. When Madeline Hartwick extended her gloved hand to Edna, the old woman took it, but still no words were exchanged.

As she moved on, Edna Burnham surveyed the silent crowd with a look both haughty and accusing. Everyone who watched had the uneasy feeling that she was searching for people who weren't there, for there was nothing left of Martha Ward's family except for Rebecca and Clara Wagner, who was slowly dying in her room at the nursing home and would never return to Blackstone again.

Edna barely glanced at Bonnie and Amy Becker as she passed them. At last she came to the marble structure in which Charles and Eleanor Connally, along with their daughter and granddaughter, had long ago been interred.

Harvey Connally's bronze coffin, bare of flowers, stood in front of the open door of the crypt; soon it would rest inside, where Harvey would sleep eternally next to his sister, Olivia.

At the head of the coffin, Lucas Iverson stood with an open Bible in his hand, though he needed no prompting to recite once more the prayers that would accompany Harvey Connally's soul to his Maker.

At the foot of the coffin stood Oliver Metcalf.

Next to him, her hand in Oliver's, stood Rebecca Morrison.

The crowd waited in silence as Edna Burnham drew close, finally stopping only a few feet from Oliver.

Her eyes fixed on Oliver for a long time, and the mourners seemed to hold their breath as they waited in tense anticipation to hear what she might say to the man about whom she had been whispering for months—the man whose reputation she had done her best to ruin.

Oliver, his face expressionless, met her granite stare, knowing that whatever she said in the next few moments would be passed from one person to another until there was no one in Blackstone who hadn't heard.

But Edna still bided her time, turning at last to Rebecca Morrison.

Rebecca Morrison, who had once humiliated her in public and now stood next to Oliver Metcalf, one of her hands in his, her face revealing nothing, her eyes clear. In her free hand she held the handkerchief Oliver had given her the day before she'd disappeared.

As she gazed first at Rebecca, and then at Oliver Metcalf, it came to Edna Burnham that the truth of what had happened inside the Asylum three days ago was never going to be revealed to her, at least not by Oliver or Rebecca.

The only other person who might have been able to tell her lay dead inside the coffin that stood in front of the mausoleum. As Lucas Iverson, the hand that held his

Bible trembling, opened his mouth to begin the service, Edna Burnham silenced him with a glance. Her gaze shifted back to Oliver. She gave him a hard appraising look, then turned to Rebecca.

The silence lengthened like a cold shadow creeping over the crowd as the citizens of Blackstone waited.

Then, as if coming to a decision, she nodded her head. "It's over," she said, resting her hand on Harvey Connally's coffin. She looked up to the Asylum, still looming atop North Hill. Though her voice rose only slightly when she spoke again, it carried easily to every corner of the cemetery. "It's time we put the past to rest." She stepped back and bowed her head as Lucas Iverson finally began to intone the last words that would be spoken over Harvey Connally.

"Ashes to ashes, dust to dust . . ."

As the prayer went on, the eyes that had been fixed on Harvey Connally's coffin shifted one by one toward the dark silhouette of the building that stood atop North Hill.

Empty at last, one of its walls shattered by the blows Oliver Metcalf had struck three days ago, it had lost its air of domination. Weakened and forlorn, stripped at last of the power it had held over Blackstone for so long. Everyone who listened to Lucas Iverson's prayer knew that Edna Burnham had, for once, finally spoken the truth.

The past, along with Harvey Connally, was finally being buried.

But it was only Oliver Metcalf who noticed the date that had been engraved on the door of his uncle's crypt.

April 24, 1997.

Until this very moment, he'd forgotten what day it was that his uncle had died.

The date of his mother's death.

The date of his own birth.

His birthday.

His forty-fifth birthday.

And the day that he had finally been released from the torture of his past.

That, he knew, had been his uncle's final gift to him.

As he stared at the date, he felt Edna Burnham standing rigidly beside him. It was only then that he realized he was not the only one staring at the date on the door of Harvey Connally's crypt.

Rebecca—and Edna Burnham—were staring at it too.

Afterword

Dear Reader,

For the past year I have lived in Blackstone, New Hampshire. Never before has a town and its citizens become so real to me. Far more than characters in a novel, the people of Blackstone have become personal friends, and as I write these words I feel an emptiness inside of me. I don't want to say good-bye to Rebecca and Oliver. I don't want to look in my rearview mirror and see North Hill and the square disappearing in the distance. I will miss my meanderings inside the library, the *Chronicle* office and, yes, even the Asylum. I shall truly miss dropping into the Red Hen for a piece of pie (pecan, of course) and a good dose of gossip. In short, I'm not sure I want to leave. But the story is over. Or, at any rate, this part of the story is over.

Writing *The Blackstone Chronicles* has been a marvelous and challenging experience. I loved being able to create a story with a beginning, a middle, and an end in a hundred pages. It was a constant challenge to sustain the suspense over a six-month period, and it was delightful to get to know my characters so well. Many of them turned out to have facets to their personalities that I knew nothing about at the beginning. And I thoroughly enjoyed bringing back characters and references from other books. It was like getting in touch with old friends—even if they were as troubled as Elizabeth Conger (who finally, after all these years, got what was coming to her!), and Melissa Holloway, whose future had worried me ever since the unfortunate events that occurred in Secret Cove in *Second Child.*

But there was also an underlying apprehension that was always with me. What would happen if I got ill and couldn't finish the series? What if I created a plot problem in an already published part that couldn't be resolved in a later part? There were times when I was editing one book, writing another, and proofreading a third. Federal Express and my modem received a real workout. Artwork had to be reviewed, maps drawn, and chronologies and genealogies updated constantly. I'm sure there are those who are still wondering why it was Charles Connally rather than Jonas Connally who built the mansion on the hill. Well, it seems I goofed in the first part, and said that Harvey's father built it, when I should have said his grandfather did. But as I've thought about it, I suspect that this was not an error at all, and that the mansion was built as part of the schism between Jonas Connally and his children. I'm sure there is a story there, though I'm not yet sure what it is.

I thank my lucky stars that I had a stellar group of people working close to me. My editor, Linda Grey—to whom I have dedicated the series—was forever helping me out. My agent, Jane Rotrosen Berkey, was on call to review every book to make sure the stories were holding together. My friend, Mike Sack, who has been involved in my career from the very beginning, stood by as always and kept me moving in the right direction. Also, with his expertise in psychology, he kept the denizens of the Asylum exquisitely maniacal. My staff, Robb Miller and Lori Dickenson, spent hours maintaining detailed files that kept track of the minutiae of the people, places, and things in Blackstone.

The production of a serial novel is a major undertaking for a publisher. Far more major, I suspect, than any of us knew a year ago. A lot of the company's resources must be funneled into the project for a very long period of time. Ballantine/Fawcett as well as Random House stood behind the project all the way. Alberto Vitale, Chairman of Random House, was supportive from the start, when only he and Linda Grey knew what we were about to attempt. Within months, the group involved in Blackstone quickly grew. My copy editor, Peter Weissman, performed beyond the call of duty in keeping track of the details of Blackstone from one volume to another, ready to review each book on a moment's notice, as did managing editor Mark Rifkin. The advertising and publicity departments worked many hard hours to get the word out that Blackstone was coming, and the sales force worked with every book outlet in the country to assure that each book would be on the stands when it was due, so we didn't have different parts popping up at different times and in different places, creating chaos at the Red Hen.

The booksellers themselves performed yeoman service in making sure you could get each new part as quickly as it was released, which is no easy task when thousands of books arrive in their stores and warehouses every month.

Very special thanks go to Ellen Key Harris and Phebe Kirkham, who developed the Blackstone Web site and thereby provided many of us, myself included, with a unique experience. The Blackstone site has become a regular hangout over the last six months, and it has brought an entire new dimension to the form of the novel. Some of you may have noticed that our favorite waitress at the Red Hen diner, Velma Perkins, didn't appear in the first few books. That is because Velma was Ellen Harris's invention, and I didn't meet her until the rest of you did. By the time I'd dropped into the Red Hen a few times, Velma had become totally real to me, and soon she began showing up in the books. (I guess I stole her from you, Ellen. Sorry about that!) There are a few others I met at the Red Hen, new people who have moved to town and who are now working at the bank or assisting Oliver at his office, who aren't mentioned in the books, but you know who you are, and know how much I've appreciated getting to know you. I hope all of you keep your ear to the ground, because I have a feeling there's a lot more going on in Blackstone than any of us yet knows. As you can see, the Web site has brought you, my readers, close to me, and I have enjoyed being able to talk to you, not only at the Red Hen but through e-mail as well. The cyber-Blackstone added a whole new dimension not only to the experience of reading the novel but of writing it as well. I thank all of you who participated.

Stephen King not only opened the door for me to write a serial novel but has also been incredibly supportive throughout. When I felt overwhelmed by the complications, he assured me that I'd get through it and all would be well. I cannot express how much that support meant to me. Thanks again, Steve.

I know that there are a few minor errors that I made as I wrote the novel; errors I couldn't go back to fix since the parts in which they surfaced were already published. At one point, we actually called the printer to change a word as one of the books was in the midst of being printed. Sometimes, though, I was just too late, and a few goofs got through. Apparently this is inevitable when a book is being published before the last word has been written. Or maybe it's just that the renewal of the form is so recent that we haven't quite figured out how to do it yet.

Many of you have asked if I will write another serial. The answer is yes—if the story is right for the format. Many of you have also asked if there will be more of Blackstone. All I can say at this point is that I had a ball writing *The Blackstone Chronicles*, and while right now I'm not positive of anything, I wouldn't be at all surprised if sometime in the future you glance up at a book rack and see the shadow of a building sitting up on North Hill.

Thank you all for going on a six-month ride with me through the town of Blackstone. I only hope you've all enjoyed it as much as I have.

John Saul

Evil has a new name.

It moves without mercy.

It surrounds you like air.

It offers no escape.

For its dark, vaporous soul
will permeate every corner of your imagination
until there's no more breath to scream. . . .

Read on
for a chilling look at
THE PRESENCE. . . .

Prologue

LOS ANGELES

It wasn't supposed to be like this.

Everything was supposed to be getting better, not worse.

They'd promised him—everyone had promised him.

First the doctor: "If you take the pills, you'll feel better."

Then his coach: "Just try a little harder. No pain, no gain."

Even his mom: "Just take it one day at a time, and don't try to do everything at once."

So he'd taken the pills, and he'd tried harder, but also tried not to do too much. And for a while last week things had actually seemed to improve. Although smog had settled over the city so heavily that most of his friends had cut out of school early—headed for the beach, where an offshore wind might bring fresh air in from the ocean—he'd gone to all his classes. After the last bell he'd stripped out of his clothes in the locker room and donned his gym shorts before going out to the track to do the four warm-up laps that always preceded the more serious work of the high hurdles.

The event that just might, with a little more work, make him a state champion on his eighteenth birthday.

And that day last week, when he was alone on the field, the pills had at last seemed to kick in. He'd been expecting to lose his wind halfway around the first lap, but even as he came around the final turn he felt his body surging with energy, his lungs pumping air easily, his heartbeat barely above normal. On the second and third laps he'd kicked his pace up a notch, but he still felt good—*really* good. So on the fourth lap he'd gone all out, and it had been just like a few months ago, when he'd still felt great all the time. And on that one day last week he'd felt even greater than ever: his lungs had been sucking huge volumes of air, and his whole body had responded. Instead of the slow burn of pain he usually felt toward the end of the warm-up mile, his muscles had merely tingled pleasurably, his chest expanding and contracting in an easy rhythm that synched perfectly with his steady heartbeat. His whole body had been functioning in perfect harmony. He'd even taken a couple of extra laps that day, exulting in the strength of his body, euphoric that finally the pills and the exercise were working. He'd set up the hurdles then, spacing them perfectly, but setting them a little higher than usual.

He'd soared over them one after the other, clearing the crossbars easily, feeling utterly weightless as his body floated over one barricade after another.

When he'd finally started back to the locker room two hours after he'd begun, he was barely out of breath, his heart was beating easily, and his legs felt as if he'd been strolling for only half an hour instead of running and jumping full out for two.

The next day it had all crashed in on him.

A quarter of the way around the first lap he'd felt the familiar constrictions around his lungs, and his heart began pounding as if he were in the last stretch of a 10k run. He kept going, telling himself it was nothing more than a reaction from the day before, when he'd worked far harder than he should have. But by the time he'd finished the first lap, he'd known it wasn't going to work. Swerving off the hard-packed earth of the track, he'd flopped down onto the grass, rolling over to stare up into the blue of the sky, squinting against the glare of the afternoon sun. What the hell was wrong? Yesterday he'd felt great. Today he felt like an old man.

He'd refused to give in to the pain in his lungs, the pounding of his heart, the agony in his legs. When his coach had come over to find out if he was all right, he'd tossed it off, claiming he'd just gotten a cramp, then rubbed the muscles of his right calf as if to prove the lie. The coach had bought it—or at least pretended to, which was just as good—and he'd stood up and gone back to the track.

He'd made it through the four laps, but by the last one he'd only been able to maintain a pace that was little more than a fast walk.

The coach had told him to try harder or go home.

He'd tried harder, but in the end he'd gone home.

And each day it had grown worse.

Each day, he'd struggled a little harder against the pain.

The day before yesterday he'd gone to the doctor for the fourth time since New Year's, and once again the doctor hadn't been able to find anything wrong. Once again he'd answered all the questions: Yes, he was fine when he came back from Maui with his mom after New

Year's. No, his father hadn't been there; he'd gone to Grand Cayman with his new wife and their baby. No, it didn't bother him that his dad hadn't gone to Maui with them—in fact, he was glad his mom had dumped his dad, since his dad seemed to like hitting both of them when he got drunk, which had been practically every night the last couple of years before he finally left. No, he didn't hate his dad. He didn't like him much, and was glad he was gone, but he didn't hate him.

What he hated was the way he felt.

The doctor had said maybe he should see a shrink, but he wasn't about to do that. Only geeks and losers went to shrinks. Whatever was wrong, he'd get over it by himself. But during the last two days the pain had become almost unbearable. He was having nightmares, and waking up unable to breathe, and his whole body had started hurting all the time.

This afternoon, when he'd started feeling that maybe it might be better just to die if he couldn't get away from the pain, he'd cut out after school and driven around for a while until finally a cop had stopped him and given him a ticket for having a broken muffler. So now what the hell was he going to do? He couldn't afford to pay for the ticket, let alone get the damn muffler on the car fixed. Besides, what was the big deal? It didn't make that much noise, and hardly stank up the inside of the car at all. But his mom was going to give him hell for the ticket anyway, and his dad would only launch into an endless lecture about how much it costs to raise two families if he asked to borrow the money to fix the muffler.

What a goddam mess!

Turning into the tree-lined block on which he'd lived all his life, he pressed the button on the sun visor that would activate the garage door opener while he was still two houses away, and turned into the driveway just as the door opened fully. Automatically starting the game he played against himself every afternoon, he pressed the button again, trying to gauge it so that the descending garage door would barely miss the rear end of the car as he pulled it inside.

Today he missed, and the car jolted sharply as the garage door glanced off the rear bumper. So now there would be scrapes on the car and the garage door, as well as the ticket and the bad muffler.

And he still hurt.

Maybe, instead of going into the house, he'd just sit here a while.

Sit here and see what happened.

A feeling of warmth spread through him, washing away the pain he'd been enduring, and suddenly everything began to seem better.

Maybe he'd finally found the answer to his problems.

Without his mother.

Without his coach.

Even without his doctor.

The boy closed his eyes, breathed deeply, and, for the first time in weeks, felt no pain.

For the woman, the day had been no better than it had for her son, starting with an early call from her ex-husband suggesting that they renegotiate his child support payments. Translation: the bimbo he'd run off with wanted more money to spend on herself. Well, she'd disabused him of that idea pretty quickly. At noon she'd discovered that an associate who was a full year junior to her was going to get the partnership slot that should have been hers. So now she was faced with a decision: sit it out for another year, or start job hunting. But she knew the answer to that one: she wasn't going to be made a partner, ever, so she might as well start checking with the headhunters.

Then, just when things looked as though they couldn't get any worse, the doctor had called to recommend a good psychiatrist for her son. Well, before she sent him off to a shrink, she'd have him checked out by someone else. Except that the HMO probably wouldn't pay for it, and the trip to Maui at New Year's had strained the budget as far as it would go.

Still, she'd figure out something.

Turning into the driveway, she jabbed the remote on the visor, bringing the car to a complete stop as she waited for the garage door to open.

It was the noise of her son's car more than the fumes that poured out of the garage that told her that something was wrong. Slamming the gear lever into Park with one hand as she opened the door with the other, she slid out of her car and ran into the garage.

Now she could see her son slumped inside the car, his legs up on the front passenger seat, his back resting against the driver's door. His head was lolling on his chest.

Stifling a scream, she grabbed the driver's door handle.

Locked!

She ran around the car and tried the other door, then called her son's name.

Nothing!

Wait!

Had something moved inside the car?

She cupped her hands over her eyes and peered into its shadowy interior.

His chest was moving! He was still breathing!

Coughing as the fumes in the garage filled her lungs, she fumbled for the extra key that hung from a nail under the workbench, shoved open the door to the kitchen, and grabbed the phone. "My son!" she cried as soon as the 911 operator answered. "Oh, God, I need an ambulance!"

A carefully measured voice calmly asked for her address.

Her address!

Her mind was suddenly blank. "I can't—oh, God! It's—" Then it came back to her, and she blurted out a number. "On North Maple, between Dayton and Clifton. Oh, God, hurry! He locked himself in the car in the garage, and—"

"It's all right, ma'am," the calm voice broke in. "An Aid car is already on its way."

Dropping the phone on the counter, she raced back to the garage. She had to get the car open—she had to! A hammer! There used to be a sledgehammer at the end of the workbench! Squeezing between the front of her son's car and the wooden bench, she uttered a silent prayer that her ex-husband hadn't simply helped himself to the big maul. He hadn't—it was right where she remembered it. Grasping its handle with both hands, she hoisted it up, then slammed its huge metal head into the passenger window of her son's car. The safety glass shattered into thousands of tiny pieces, and instantly the woman dropped the hammer to the floor, snaked a hand through the broken window, and pulled the door open. Reaching across her son's body, she switched the ignition off, and the loud rumble of the motor died away, only to be instantly replaced by the wail of a fast-approaching siren. She grasped her son's ankles and started trying to pull him out of the car, but before she'd managed to haul him even halfway through the door, two white-clad medics were taking over, gently easing her aside as they pulled the boy out of the car and clamped an oxygen mask over his face. As he began to stir, her panic at last began to ease its grip.

"He's coming around," one of them assured her as they carried him out of the garage and put him on a stretcher. "Looks like he's going to make it okay."

Her son began struggling as the medics put him into the ambulance and started to close its rear door.

"I want to come," the woman begged. "For God's sake! He's my son!"

The door to the ambulance reopened, and the woman scrambled inside. With the siren wailing, the ambulance raced toward Cedars-Sinai Hospital, nearly twenty blocks away.

The ride seemed to take forever, with the woman watching helplessly as her son struggled against the two medics, one of whom was trying to hold the boy still while the other kept the oxygen mask pressed firmly over his nose and mouth. Clutching her son's hand, the woman tried to soothe him, and finally his struggles eased. But then, just as the ambulance pulled to a stop at the hospital's emergency entrance, she felt his hand suddenly relax in hers. His whole body went limp on the stretcher.

She heard one of the medics curse softly.

Her body went numb, and when the doors were yanked open from the outside, she climbed out of the ambulance slowly, as if she'd fallen into a trance.

The crew rushed her son into the emergency room, where a team of doctors waited to take over for the medics.

She followed the stretcher into the hospital.

Silently, she watched the doctors work, but already knew what was coming.

And in the end, she heard the same words she'd heard first from her son's doctor, then from the ambulance crew: "I don't understand—he should be doing fine!"

But her son—her sweet, handsome only son—wasn't doing fine.

Her son was dead.

In *The Presence*, John Saul— bestselling master of nineteen previous chilling works of fiction in addition to the six volumes of *The Blackstone Chronicles*—delivers his most terrifying novel to date.

Don't miss John Saul's new novel of breathtaking suspense—coming to bookstores everywhere soon!

THE PRESENCE

More tales of chilling
horror from
John Saul

GUARDIAN

A telephone rings in the dead of night with shock-ing news for single mother MaryAnne Carpenter: Her friends, the Wilkensons, are suddenly, inexplic-ably, dead, leaving MaryAnne's godchild abruptly orphaned.

But as MaryAnne rushes to the Wilkensons' ranch to embrace her young charge, disturbing questions mount. Was it an accident that killed her friends? Or murder?

Now, as winter batters the ranch with blinding, dangerous storms, a series of horrific murders bear-ing the marks of a wild animal draws closer to MaryAnne and her young family.

GUARDIAN
by John Saul
Published by Fawcett Books.
Available in your local bookstore.

THE HOMING

by

JOHN SAUL

Karen Spellman is having a sweet homecoming. After years of living in Los Angeles, the pretty young widow is returning to Pleasant Valley with her daughters to marry her high school sweetheart.

But something sinister awaits her. Long ago a shadowy menace, since forgotten, stalked Pleasant Valley.

Now Karen's homecoming will become a confrontation with terror as she battles to protect her daughters from a preternatural force that must satisfy its thirst for innocent prey.

THE HOMING
by John Saul
Published by Fawcett Books.
Available in your local bookstore.

BLACK LIGHTNING

by

JOHN SAUL

For five years Seattle journalist Anne Jeffers has pursued the horrifying story of a sadistic serial killer's bloody reign, capture, trial, and appeal— crusading to keep the wheels of justice churning toward the electric chair.

Now the day of execution has come. A convicted killer will meet his end. Anne believes her long nightmare is over. But she's dead wrong....

BLACK LIGHTNING
by John Saul
Published by Fawcett Books.
Available in bookstores everywhere.